OFF WITH HER HEART

Amy Dale

The characters and events in this book are fictitious. Any similarity to real persons, living or dead, is coincidental and not intended by the author.

Published by Catalytix, Woodland Park, CO 80863

First Edition: May 2013

Cover Design: Carter Martin

ISBN-13: HC 978-0-9892111-0-9   PB 978-0-9892111-1-6

Printed in the United States of America

For my husband Jon who believes in me more than I believe in myself.

Anna, Eli, Shae and Aspen. May you always be able to find your way back to Wonderland.

My amazing Kickstarter backers:

A. K. Tosh
Aaron Curtis
Aaron Deckler
Aaron McHugh
Alex
Alex Burton
Alex Dompe
Allan Branch
Allen
Amanda Roberts
Amy Kincaid
Andrew Buckman
Andrew Wartman
Andy Traub
Angie Anderson
Anj Pettigrew
Anne Evans
Annmarie Bianchi
Anthony Vilgiate
Archie Winningham
Ashley Elizabeth Sherwood
Becky C
Ben Kvanli
Brad Dancer
Brian Hobson
Brian Roszkowski
Caeldwyn
Caleb Sledd
Candice Bailey
Carla
Carlos Enrique Uribe
Casper Wong

Cassie Newkirk
Chad Johnston
Charles Anderson
Charley Tam
Chelsea Seibert
Chris
Chris Lin
Chris Puckett
Christophe Boutter
Christopher Ferebee
Chuck
Dan
Dan Miller
Dawn Oshima
Deanna McNeil
Dustin
Felicity Dale
Freddie Palesano
Ganji
Geoffrey Ford
George Keng
Gill
Grace Bell
Greg
Greg Sailors
Halil Gokdal
HanoverFiste
Hayden Lockstead
Heather Bonney
Ivan Yagolnikov
James
James Husum
James Woosley
Jamie Goudie
Jamie Linde
Jamie Scammahorn

Jason Sperber
Jeff Loper
Jennifer M Zeiger
Jeremiah
Jim Gadberry
Jim Ryan
John Abel
John Bergquist
John-Erik Moseler
José Manuel Moyano Hidalgo
Joy Oram
Julie Wenzel
Justin Hall
Justin Lukasavige
Justin Macumber
Kailah Brost
Kander Judy
Karolyn muse
Kat
Kathleen Cotton
Ken Ott
Kevin Miller
Kim Gardner
Kristian
Kristy Lourance
Lana
Lane
Laura Werner
Laurie MacDougall
Lee maynard
Leibowitz
Leslie
Levi Smith
Lianne
Lindsay Mehrkens
Marjorie-Ann Lacharite

Mark & Amy Polson
Mark Bovee
Mark Daniel Miller
Mark Jones Jr.
Mark Weaver
Mary Harden Rudisill
Mary Rose Cloninger
Matt Daley
Matthew Bear-Fowler
Matthew Dale
Melanie Hart
Michael Bell
Michael Dalton
Michael Fuqua
Michael Hyatt
Michael Robinson
Michelle Clements
Mike G
Morgan Snyder
Neubian
Nic Bovee
Paul
Paul Giffney
R.J.Noble
Rebecca Thornberry
Rocco Capra
Roger Bianchi
Ron Sheehan
Royce Harrell
Sam Jolman
Sarah
Sarah K
Scarlett Millsaps
Scott P Barnes
Scott Shipley
Seth Godin

Shard73
Shari Jones
Sinsofangels
Stasi Eldredge
Stephanie Shell
Steve
Steve Dale
Stuart Holcombe
Susan Lewis
Sven Patrick Larsen
Tammie Gonzalez
Tara Mansbridge Owens
Terry Penn
Thad Puckett
The Pikes Peak Guy
Timothy
Todd
Todd Anderson
Tom James Allen Jr
Vincent Deloso
Welfringer Tom
Wendy Sutter-Staas
Zoe Tsang

CHAPTER 1

WILLIAM and Elizabeth Pennington were new money. They lived in a small village in the south of England comprised primarily of poverty with a healthy dose of old money. William's father owned a shop where he built pocket watches. He was a gifted watchmaker and he taught William all he knew. Although he put in long hours and worked as hard as any man, their family barely scraped by. When William took over after his father's death, he made a few simple changes and began to market his watches. After a few years of working hard with his new bride, Elizabeth, something happened. Pennington watches became all the rage. They were put into shops all over England. Everyone who was anyone had to have a Pennington watch. Even people with no money or station were setting aside money in hopes of one day buying a Pennington.

Elizabeth was proud of her young husband and eager to blend into the high society circles. She had been raised by her aunt who was insistent that she marry well. Aunt Agnes disapproved of William and disowned Elizabeth as soon as she learned of their engagement. Elizabeth planned to prove her aunt wrong by becoming the most important (and wealthiest) socialite in southern England.

About a year after their fortunes started changing, Elizabeth discovered she was pregnant. She and William were both elated. All the ladies with influence in the village were pleased to see such an up and coming couple becoming a family.

Katherine Abigail Pennington was born right on time. She was a rather chubby baby with a shock of black hair that seemed as though it was always reaching to the sky for something. Elizabeth's friends (if you could call them that...it might be more appropriate to say "the ladies she wanted to impress") were all amazed with what a well behaved baby Katherine was. Indeed, she hardly cried. She would sit and just look out at the world. She studied things quietly.

William and Elizabeth were both delighted with Katherine until she started to speak. As she learned to speak, she began to express herself and assert herself in a way that was not at all acceptable.

Elizabeth did love her child, but, in truth, she mainly enjoyed the attention and accolades that Katherine earned her. When Katherine began to be more of an embarrassment than an asset, Elizabeth found that her fondness for her was waning.

William wasn't very involved in the parenting as was the way of most men in that time. He simply followed Elizabeth's lead in how he should respond to Katherine.

Katherine was naturally curious and bright. She was constantly chastised for touching things she ought not touch or asking questions she needn't be concerned about. She would sit and look at books for hours, even before she could read. Once she was old enough to read on her own, she would sit surrounded by piles of heavy tomes, smiling happily as she turned the pages. Elizabeth could only imagine what the ladies in her league would have to say about this.

Katherine was very intuitive and realized at a young age that she was not what her parents hoped for. She tried very hard to become the person they wanted her to be. She tried to sit like a lady instead of running wild in the field chasing butterflies. She tried to read less and sew more.

But there came a day when Katherine decided that she didn't like the girl her parents wanted her to be. She was about seven years old and she was walking through the village with her mother. She spotted an old man. He was lying on the ground with a cup next to him. His clothes were tattered and covered in filth. His hair was matted and falling out in places. Katherine was born with a larger than normal dose of compassion. She ran to him and put her hand on his face. She smiled at him, and he smiled back with the few teeth he had left. She rubbed his matted hair and turned to look up at her mother.

Elizabeth was embarrassed and appalled. The ladies league she was involved in donated money to all sorts of charities and humanitarian organizations, but would never consider touching a person like this themselves.

Katherine could see her mother's embarrassment and desperation to get her away from this filthy creature. She decided at that moment that she didn't like this girl that her mother wanted her to be. She leaned into the man's face and whispered.

"There is still magic in you. I can feel it." She stood and walked away from her mother. The old man sat up and smiled so wide he felt his cheeks stretching in a way that he had nearly forgotten.

Elizabeth gathered up her skirts and hurried off after Katherine, chastising her all the way home.

* * *

When she had grown to the age of twelve, Katherine had become settled in who she was. She realized that she was different, and it seemed that no matter how hard she tried or didn't try, her parents were never going to accept her. She didn't want to need their love. She wanted to be independent and free, but the desire for their approval, for the feeling that she was accepted and loved just as she was, just wouldn't seem to leave her. She found safety and guidance from books. She buried herself in them.

Katherine had few friends. The ones that claimed to be her friends were only hoping for an invite to her parents' legendary parties that involved candies shipped in from Paris, live music, and sometimes fireworks. Katherine was smart enough to realize this, and she found it simpler and less painful to be alone. She wasn't just smart, she was also fairly attractive. Her hair was dark as a raven and had finally decided to hang straight. Her features were fine and well centered. When she thought hard, she scrunched her face in a way that her mother said was absolutely deplorable. She didn't think of herself as pretty. No one had told her otherwise.

She spent most of her time in the family library or by the stream near the house. She would sit for hours beside the little ivy-covered bridge reading, playing solitaire, or watching the insects and animals that played around the stream. While the other girls were learning to sit for tea and embroider a tea towel, Katherine was dancing in the meadow alone. She was of the unusual opinion that there was more to life than having tea.

She was very much alone in her life. She thought her parents probably did love her, but they were very busy and baffled by a child that didn't act like every other girl in the county. Ms. Glass was

Katherine's one love. She had been hired when Katherine was about four years old. Her only job had been to take care of Katherine and make sure she didn't interfere with the Penningtons' social events. She was a round woman with perpetually rosy cheeks and a laugh that sounded more like a chipmunk chattering than a large woman chuckling. She gave the best hugs, and Katherine always looked forward to being gathered up in her arms and squeezed till she thought she would never breathe again.

Ms. Glass had her hands full trying to get Katherine to put on social graces and act as she was supposed to, but her love for little Katherine let her get by with more than the Penningtons would have liked. It's not that Katherine didn't try to please them, but sometimes she found that trying made things even worse. Like the New Year's party that the Pennington's held every year. One year Katherine decided she would learn all the dances and etiquette and try very hard to become one of the crowd. She injured at least three people on the dance floor, spilled tea on the matriarch of the town, and told the priest that she didn't believe anyone was truly honest — including him. Her parents were appalled and told her that she would not come to any more parties unless she learned to become invisible. She did. One might spot Katherine Pennington at one of the famous parties, but you would never remember seeing her. She became a piece of furniture.

At one point, Mrs. Pennington attempted to fire Ms. Glass. Katherine had been at school and a boy about her age pulled her black hair like reins and told her that she would be a better fit as a Pennington if she were a horse in their stable. Katherine pushed him in the mud. The teacher discussed the issue with Ms. Glass. Ms. Glass did the unthinkable and defended Katherine. She even suggested the boy (who was from a very prestigious family) be punished. The teacher then

5

discussed things with Mrs. Pennington, who did the right thing and apologized for her disturbed daughter.

When Elizabeth arrived home, she informed both Ms. Glass and Katherine that Ms. Glass would be leaving. Katherine ran into the garden in full view of the new neighbors and started screaming at the top of her lungs and pulling her long dark hair. The adults followed, trying to quiet her. It wasn't until her mother whispered that Ms. Glass would stay that Katherine finally grew quiet and walked back into the house. Mrs. Pennington laughed uncomfortably and waved in the direction of the neighbors gawking nearby. Katherine hated giving her mother a new reason to despise her, but she couldn't lose Ms. Glass.

And so Katherine's life continued as it always had, living in a land that felt completely foreign to her, even though she'd lived there all her life. It wouldn't always be this way. A day was soon to come when Ms. Glass lost Katherine as she knew her. Katherine, however, was reborn in a way, to a land that felt more like home than anything she'd known.

CHAPTER 2

KATHERINE was sitting on the floor of the library with books piled around her and a cup of tea balanced on her knee. She was attempting to pick a new book to read. This was always a long and drawn-out event. She would turn each book over in her hand and read little bits out of each one. She would often be in the library most of the day with Ms. Glass bringing her meals there on the floor.

She heard a sound of shuffling feet and jostling material. She looked up to see her mother standing in the doorway. She had always thought that her mother resembled a bird more than a human. She was tall and thin and her nose, while not large, was much more like a beak than a nose. Standing in the doorway now, holding her skirt up, her skinny ankles and pointed shoes poking out, Katherine half expected her to squawk instead of speak.

"Katherine Abigail! What are you doing here?" she asked, as though surprised that she lived in the same house.

"I'm attempting to choose which book to read next, but it's — ," she started.

"Yes, well, you will have to clear out of the library for today and do your playing another day." She waved her hands as though shooing an insect.

"Why?" Katherine rarely made things easy. Mrs. Pennington sighed and tilted her head.

"Well, if you must know, the Ladies of the League are meeting here today, and they requested that we have tea in the library so that we could discuss our donations." She smoothed her dress nervously.

"Donations?" Katherine asked.

"Yes, we are donating some of our books to help start a public library. So that everyone may have access to books." She smiled, pleased with herself.

"You are giving away our books?" Katherine felt panic rising in her chest. She loved the idea of giving to others, but picturing herself on the floor of a public building surrounded by piles of books attempting to choose what to read next just didn't seem fitting, even for someone like Katherine.

"Calm down, dear; we are only giving away some of our sets of reference books. I know how much you love your books," Mrs. Pennington stated. Katherine felt that this was the largest and grandest expression of affection that her mother had ever given her. Carried away in the moment, she jumped to her feet and flew at her, embracing her. She could almost hear feathers ruffling as her mother hopped back a step and threw her hands up to guard herself from Katherine's embrace. She smiled, but it wasn't genuine, and Katherine knew she had crossed some imaginary line that she was supposed to stay behind. She felt the pain of the rejection in her chest like a tiny stab wound.

"Thank you, mother. I'll just clear up my mess and go out for a walk," she managed to say. Mrs. Pennington nodded and shuffled off to make sure Ms. Glass was getting things prepared for the onslaught of skirts, gossip, and tea.

Katherine picked up the books one by one, lovingly stroked the spine, and set them all back in their empty slots around the room. She kept one in her hand, a tale of an adventure in a faraway land. She would read this one today. She gave the room one last look, then headed to the kitchen to put away her tea cup. She walked in to her mother chirping directions so frantically that she wondered when she was drawing a breath. Ms. Glass glanced up and grinned, then shot a quick wink at Katherine as she took her cup from her hand.

Katherine walked down the hall clutching her stomach. Nothing was wrong physically, but she felt the need to somehow hold her insides in. She didn't want the feelings on the inside to slip out, to reveal the pain she allowed her parents to inflict on her.

She stopped at the hall closet and grabbed her playing cards (a Christmas gift from Ms. Glass). As she headed toward the front door, something made her pause. The front parlor had a large grand mirror that leaned against the wall. It had belonged to a great-great aunt of some sort and had a huge elaborate gold frame. She was used to walking past and seeing her other self walking by inside the sparkling frame. Today the mirror seemed wrong. It looked as though it were full of fog. The curtains had been opened this morning, just as they had every morning, and sun was streaming into the room. Katherine walked closer to investigate. She caught a glimpse of her own reflection through the fog. She had a strange feeling.

She reached her hand up to touch the glass, but it went straight through and into the fog. She pulled it back in a moment of terror and looked behind her, as though any second someone was going to catch her and reprimand her or laugh at how ridiculous she was being. But

9

alas, it is difficult to walk away when something so miraculous is happening. She plunged both arms into the fog and one leg stepped forward. As her other leg attempted to follow, her foot caught on the frame of the mirror, which apparently was still quite solid. She felt herself falling back into the parlor, but something wrapped around her wrist and pulled her forward. She felt the mirror fall and turned to see it shatter into a thousand pieces. She was horrified. Her mother would be furious. Another bad mark on Katherine's far-from-perfect score card. But that thought would have to wait. Now she was more concerned about what had grabbed her and pulled her through the mirror.

CHAPTER 3

KATHERINE looked down at her wrist and found a rather large toothless snake had wrapped his tail around it. She shook the serpent off and backed away. Her eyes widened, and she rubbed her wrist absently.

"Are you hurt, miss?" the snake asked. His head tilted and his unblinking eyes stared up at her with concern.

Katherine looked long and hard at the serpent. She thought she must have hit her head rather hard or addled her brain in some way. For a moment, the snake had seemed like something more than a snake, as though it were speaking to her.

"You are most welcome! Now, what is it that we should be calling you when we are in need of calling you?" he spoke again.

Katherine looked intently at the snake, then surveyed her surroundings. She was in a vast meadow surrounded by forest. The colors were more vivid than any she'd ever seen. The trees were unrecognizable to her, and some of them hung with deep purple and turquoise fruit. She had read enough in her short life to realize that she had crossed over to another world somehow. The snake cleared his throat. Katherine shook herself. She realized that she still had not responded.

"My name is Kather—" she stopped herself before the rest of the name could escape her mouth. She had always preferred the name Katy, but her mother insisted that it was completely inappropriate. "My name is Katy." She curtsied. "And what is your name, kind sir?"

"My name is Billingswaith, but I am thinking that is too much of name for such a small mouth as yours. So you should be calling me Waith." He grinned a huge toothless grin and bowed his head low. Had she not been so disoriented, this would have been enough to have her rolling on the floor with laughter. She came back to her thoughts and looked behind her where the frame of the grand mirror lay covered with shards of broken glass. The snake looked at her with concern.

"Are you very much yourself?" he asked. The question caused her to pause.

"Yes, yes, I think I am," she smiled. She had long dreamt of running away to the worlds in her books, but seeing that the mirror had shattered, she wondered what that could mean. Perhaps this was a second chance to find a place where she belonged and didn't bring so much grief to those around her. But she knew nothing about this world. So, for the moment, she clung tightly to hope and pushed fear out of her heart.

"You seem not pleased that you have lost your way in, but do not be so...for, you see, you are already in." He was pleased with the wisdom he offered her.

"It's just that I fear I may have lost my way out too."

The snake looked at her in complete confusion. "Way out? Such a strange way she speaks." He shook his head, then made himself taller and looked into her eyes.

"Come along and follow after me. The Queen is expecting you."

"The Queen? Expecting me? I'm afraid you must have me confused with someone else!"

The snake narrowed his lidless eyes. "Oh, you mean someone else who appears as if from nowhere into the Vast Meadowlands, with hair as dark as a raven, and will arrive on this the fifteenth of Millvan?" He tilted his head toward her.

"But how did you know all that? Do you mean you knew I was coming?"

"The Aphid foretold."

"The Aphid?" she asked.

"He's a very powerful seer. His name is Prontil. He lives at the palace, too. He foretold of the Queen's new daughter." He gestured toward Katy with his head. "He said you would be born of smoke and glass. We have never had a child come to us this way. We thought Prontil might be losing it, but I come just in case every year. He knew the very day you would arrive (but not the year) and I was here to witness your birth just as he said. And it's a good thing too. You nearly fell back into the land of shadows. So now I will bring you to your new home," he explained.

"Wait, Queen's daughter? She thinks I am her daughter?" she asked.

"Oh, but you are. Somehow when you landed at first breath, you landed in quite the wrong self. Did you ever feel like a stranger in your own skin?" he asked.

"Well...yes, actually. Quite frequently." He nodded as though he already knew this would be her answer.

"Come along, Miss Katy. It's time to get home."

CHAPTER 4

KATY followed Waith at an easy pace through the meadows.

"Where are we?" she asked.

"The Vast Meadowlands, which, as you can see, are surrounded by the Circling Forest." Katy picked up her steps a pace or two and walked alongside Waith.

"But, I mean, this country, this land...where am I? How did I get here?" Waith looked up at her thoughtfully.

"This land is a land of wonder. It is ever changing and ever the same. It has no name that I know of. The different regions are named, but we are not named as one. As to how you got here, I am suspecting that you know much more of that than I." She continued her surveying of the area and noticed more and more things that were unfamiliar to her, and yet somehow she felt very at ease and unafraid.

As they came into the forest, she had much more trouble keeping up with Waith. He slithered easily under the brush, while she fought and pushed her way through stubborn tree branches and bushes. Occasionally she would find herself at a standstill watching something in amazement, like the little bushes that looked like small pines but would shake their needles and stand up. She could see then that they were shaped a bit like tiny ostriches. Waith would call her name and get her back on track. He assured her that there would be plenty of time in the future for her to explore all the surrounding areas.

When they neared the edge of the forest, the light turned deeper blue. Katy noticed movement to her right and turned in time to see two green eyes staring at her. Just as quickly they were gone, and she couldn't get a glimpse of what or who had been watching her.

"What was that?" she asked Waith.

"That was Degrit." He answered without looking back. "Just a village boy about your age. He lives in a home not far from here, but he seems to feel more full of happiness in the forest. It is where he is most to be found." Katy looked again, but saw nothing.

At last, the woods relented. Waith and Katy came out of the trees and into the courtyard of a palace. Katy gazed up in wonder. The palace was breathtaking. The stone was something she had never seen. It was similar to limestone, except veins of silver and gold ran through it. The roof was tiled with something similar to sapphire. It almost matched the sky in places, and the clouds seemed to float not only above the roof, but in it as well. She stood, mouth open and eyes wide. Waith chuckled.

"Are you not having palaces in the land of shadows?" he asked. Katy's parents had taken her to a palace when she was very young. She remembered it as being very cold and foreboding, quite the opposite of this piece of art which seemed so warm and inviting.

"Palaces, yes, but nothing like this...at all." Waith raised himself up to her level.

"Ah, yes, crafted by our last artist nearly two hundred years ago. It is beautiful. Come along, miss." Her feet began to follow him again,

15

although her eyes were reluctant to leave the palace.

As they came closer, the doors caught Katy's eyes. They were enormous and carved with more sapphire-like stone and a deep red wood that intertwined. It created a design that was more intricate, and at the same time more simple, than anything she'd experienced.

Land of Wonder, she thought to herself.

There were no guards, no guns or swords. Various animals and creatures were milling around in the courtyard. They all stopped and stared as Katy walked past. Waith slithered to the door and without any effort on his part, the doors opened.

They walked through the doors together. The first thing that struck Katy was the light. It seemed that there was almost more sunlight inside the palace than outside. There were great dangling crystals that hung from the ceiling and emanated light. It wasn't a chandelier. These were more like single strands that hung about randomly all over the ceiling of the palace. They brightened as living beings came near them and then slowly faded when the room was left empty.

A small brown rabbit sat on a purple velvet stool near the door. He sat up tall when he noticed them.

"Please alert your majesty that Katylove is here," Waith said. The rabbit said nothing but hopped off the chair and scampered away immediately.

"We should be waiting here," Waith said. He led Katy to a room which she quickly realized was a library. It wasn't too big in circumference, but as she looked up, the ceiling seemed so far away she couldn't even confidently identify it. The crystals hung on walls between bookshelves in this room. The shelves were crammed with books that went as far up as Katy could see. There were two large comfy chairs. Waith slithered into one and invited her to do the same.

As she did she asked, "How do you get to the higher books?" Waith looked up as though this were the first time he had thought of the question.

"I should think you just eat a bit of mushroom," he stated as though this should clear up all the confusion. "Ah, yes, look." He pointed with his tail to a corner of the room. There was a tall log leaned against the wall, with mushrooms growing from it. She was about to question him further when they heard the sound of footsteps coming near. Waith slithered out of the chair and stood tall. Katy followed him.

Two women came around the corner, both of them stunning. The first was tall and slender. Her skin was so pale it almost seemed to glow. Her hair was golden, with occasional strands that sparkled like diamonds in it and fell in long ringlets around her shoulders. Her eyes were as blue as the tiles on the roof or the carvings on the door. She was young, not much older than Katy. She came bounding in and nearly bowled Katy over with a hug. Katy hugged her back a bit awkwardly. She saw the second woman behind the first, waiting for her turn to embrace Katy. She was very like the first, but much older. Her eyes were kinder and less mischievous. Her hair was deep brown, with sections of pure silver running through it. It was pulled up in a sort of bun, and a small tiara peeked up from the top of her head.

"Oh, Katylove! At last you're here!!" The girl pushed her back by her shoulders to look at her. "You are like nothing I've ever seen...so beautiful." Katy felt blood rush to her cheeks as she tried to find words. She only managed to get out a quiet "thank you."

The second woman, who must be the Queen, came and stood across from Katy. She took Katy's chin in her hand and looked deep into her eyes.

"Oh, my dear, we are so glad you made it to us," she said. Her voice was soft and full of kindness. "We have been awaiting your arrival for such a long time." She saw Katy's face full of bewilderment. "I'm sorry, dear, this must be very overwhelming for you." She gently pushed Katy back into the chair behind her and knelt next to her. "I am certain that Waith has attempted to inform you all he can. But I shall tell you again and try to set your mind at ease. I am your mother, and this is your sister, Eisley. Your arrival was foretold some twelve years ago. You were to arrive on the fifteenth of Millvan, but we did not know the year. It could not be seen. So each year, we have sent Waith out to wait for you. Eisley was three when the foretelling came, and for many years she would run to the Meadow with Waith, hoping to be the one to greet you. We had begun to give up hope. Twelve years is a very long time. Your father never gave up, though. He died four years ago and the last thing he said to me was 'tell my Katylove that I am so sorry to have missed her.' We hoped, hoped with all our hearts that you would get to come to us before we were all gone." The Queen sighed deeply. She whispered, "And, at last, you have. You are really here with us."

"I am very glad to be here," Katy said. It was all she could manage. She was confused and excited and emotional and unsure. "But are you certain it is me you have waited for?"

Eisley laughed a laugh that would have certainly been worth a stern lecture from her bird-mother in the land of shadows, as Waith called it.

"We have never been more certain about anything, Katylove. You are you, and you are more you now than you have ever been. And, of course, I would know my sister in a heartbeat."

"Oh, dearest, do not doubt that this is your true lineage. We prayed that you would be looked after in the land of shadows. I hope your life journey has not been too difficult thus far," the Queen said.

Katy realized that she was still clutching tightly to her book and the worn pack of cards that were in her left hand. She thought of Ms. Glass. "It's been fine. I had an angel to look after me."

CHAPTER 5

KATY had spent the first twelve years of her life wishing time away. Now she felt as though she were pulling back hard on the reins in a desperate attempt to slow it down. She was fifteen now. The three years she had spent in what she affectionately called Wonderland would have been a dream come true if she had ever dared to dream such beautiful dreams.

Her mother and sister were as wonderful as they had first seemed. They showered her with love and affection, and were sensitive enough to notice when she needed to be alone.

The Queen would often say, "Remember, Eisley dear, she has not been surrounded by love as you have. We must be certain not to smother her with it."

The memories of the Shadowlands had all but disappeared in such a place. When Katy had first arrived, she lived in fear of being discovered as a fraud or of all the love toward her leaving when they really got to know her. Katy was someone special and cherished here. The kindness and affection from her mother and sister, and even Waith, had begun to heal broken places in her heart. Her hair, she quickly came to understand, was something of a novelty in Wonderland. No one had ever seen hair like hers (black as a raven), and it made her even more of a miracle to the inhabitants of the land.

She had lessons daily with Waith. He taught her all the things she would need to know to someday rule Wonderland. Between the laws and etiquette of the land being introduced, she also had to learn the basics about the plants and creatures she would encounter.

She had already had a few close encounters with creatures that she didn't realize were dangerous — like the snawlish, which is an adorable little water creature similar to a sea horse, but with larger eyes. They seem to be very friendly, but are just waiting for the precise moment to sink their tiny teeth into the webs of your fingers. Their venom is so powerful and fast-acting that you would not even have time to call for help. Waith had discovered Katy leaning over the pond and allowing them to dance amongst her fingers as she dangled them in the water. He grabbed her ankle and pulled her out so fast that her knees bled. Once she discovered the danger he had saved her from, she was really very grateful.

Waith was a kind and patient teacher, and he and Katy grew to love and antagonize each other very much. They spent the mornings in the palace going over books and laws and the ways of the land. They would walk through the great halls of the palace. Waith would brag about the sparse art that lined the walls, tapestries so threadbare they seemed desperate to unravel. He taught her that artists in Wonderland were very rare — the last one had been nearly two hundred years ago. When artists were discovered, they would devote their life to giving beauty to the land. They would not marry or have a family, they would create. They were held in almost as high esteem as the royal family. Waith had high hopes that another would come along soon.

Every day Waith and Katy took a walk to see what they might see. Waith had discovered that this was the best way to teach Katy about the wildlife in Wonderland. He would point out different plants or creatures and explain all about them. Most were harmless, some were friendly, and a few were deadly.

One particular day, the walk had gone rather late and the sky was beginning to darken. Katy saw eyes peering at her through the trees, and she was taken back to that first day walking through the Circling Forest. Those curious green eyes that had vanished.

"Waith, do we really have to go back now? Can't we just go a bit further into the forest before we turn back?" she asked. Waith opened his mouth in a wide toothless yawn.

"My dear Miss Katy, I fear I am being far too tired to venture any further today."

"Can I stay out for just a bit longer alone? I promise I won't touch any plants or creatures that I'm not familiar with." She looked at him with big pleading eyes. "Besides, we covered this area a hundred times. Isn't it time you let me go out on my own?" He let out a heavy sigh, and she knew that she had won.

"Oh...I suppose I can't be with you every moment. Be back before the moon is settled in the sky." She kissed his scaly cheek.

"Thank you, Waith. I'll be careful, I promise," she shouted as she ran into the forest in the direction of those eyes.

* * *

Katy had been fighting her way through the woods for more than twenty minutes, looking for the forest boy, and was ready to call it a night. She turned back in the direction of the palace and batted a branch out of her way. Suddenly an unfamiliar hand clasped her wrist and took off with her hand in his. Her heart pounded in her chest. She had to run to keep up with the stranger. His grip was tight, but not painful. They ran between trees, and Katy squinted to get a good look at him when the moonlight streamed between the trees.

"I wanna show you something!" he shouted. She realized with relief that this was the boy she had been searching for moments ago. She struggled to keep her feet under her. They came to a sudden stop just at the edge of the forest. They were staring out over the Vast Meadowlands. Katy started to speak, but the boy put his finger to his lips and pointed toward the meadow.

She looked him over for a moment. He was just a little taller than she. His hair was golden and short, but wild, as though all the strands were pointing in different directions at once. He had no shoes and wore only the simple pants of a peasant. His green eyes she had seen before. They seemed to be full of light, even in darkness. He was staring intently at the Meadowlands.

She gazed out, squinted, and in moments began to see lights all over the meadow, floating, flying, and hovering.

"Fireflies," she whispered. "We had something like this..." she stopped short when she realized that all of the lights had begun to change color: blue, green, yellow, purple, orange, colors unlike any she'd seen. She breathed deeply in awe. The boy took her hand and put his finger to his lips once again. He began to step forward slowly and carefully so they wouldn't scare the creatures away. She followed willingly.

She tried to get a close look at them as she walked in amongst them. All she could see were the lights. When they had walked for quite a while, the boy pointed out and all around. They were in the middle of the meadow, not far from where the shards of the mirror must have fallen. They were surrounded by the sparkling lights. She squeezed his hand with excitement.

"It's so beautiful," Katy whispered. She looked out in amazement, but she could feel him looking only at her. He let go of her hand and turned to face her.

"Watch this," he said. He took off running at top speed yelling as loud as he could and the lights shot off in every direction, but they left behind a glowing trail. The meadow was a sea of light trails of all colors. The boy turned to her and laughed.

"Touch one," he said. She reached out to the orange trail that hung in the sky near her arm. Her fingers glowed with an orange light. She pulled her hand away and still it glowed. The boy was running wild through the colors. He stopped in front of her, covered from head to toe in glowing lights. "Better hurry, it doesn't last long." That was all the invitation she needed.

She ran like wild, jumping, rolling, trying to reach every color she could see. They laughed and ran and compared stripes of light. The colors slowly faded from the sky but lingered on their skin and clothes.

"They're called fleets," he said. "They're tiny creatures. You can rarely see them past their light, unless they are dying and their light is dim. They leave light trails when they're frightened." He ran his fingers through his multi-colored hair nervously.

"I'm Katy," she said, and held her hand out to him. He laughed and shook her hand.

"I know who you are. I've heard stories of you since I was born. My mother always hoped that she would be the one to teach you the ways of a princess." He looked into the sky as though searching for something. "She was a teacher in the palace before she died." His eyes

24

became glassy.

"I'm so sorry," she said. "What happened?"

He pulled blades of grass from the ground as he spoke. "She was thrown from a horse. The healer was slow in coming, and it was too late when she arrived." He sighed. "After she left, my father was...affected. We loved her. She had a heart big enough for more love than most creatures can contain." Katy felt unsure of how to respond. She had never met anyone so ready to be so honest and open about his life. He looked into her eyes for a moment, then back into the distance. "My father is dead inside. He works at the palace in the stables. It's what he's always done. It was one of the horses he trained that threw my mother. He can't forgive himself, and he can't forget. He's reminded everyday. He's gone all day, and when he comes home he tries to talk to me, but I can see how painful it is for him. I usually pretend to have something else to do. I can sense his relief when I head for the door. That is why I'm at home in the forest." He gazed at her for a moment. "I saw you the day you arrived." He looked down and scratched behind his ear. "I'd never seen anything like you. Hair like a raven and lips like bloodwood."

Katy blushed. "Bloodwood?" she asked.

"It's a type of wood. When it's all polished, it looks like blood. Some people don't like it, but I think it's beautiful." He looked into her eyes for a brief moment, then went back to studying the grass intently.

"Is that what's on the door of the palace?" she asked.

"Yes. It's mixed with sky stone to remind us that we are human, but there is also so much more to us than blood and bones."

She nodded silently. "I know you were there that first day. I saw you. Well, just your eyes. I asked Waith about you and he told me that you were a boy my age, but I never saw you again...till now. Everytime I heard a sound in the bushes I'd search for you. I know that Waith told me, but I can't remember your name. I'm sorry."

He smiled. "It's all right. It's Degrit." He stood and held out his hand to help her up. She took it and hopped up off the damp grass. "Come on. I'll get you back to the palace."

"Thanks," she said. He led her to the edge of the forest just outside the courtyard of the palace. She turned to him to thank him for the magic of that evening, for sharing his story with her, for being so open and kind, but he had vanished again. She walked into the palace alone, not sure whether she was still glowing or if it was just happiness radiating from her skin.

CHAPTER 6

"KATYLOVE, wake up."

Katy rolled over and forced her eyes open. Eisley was standing over her with an excited grin on her face.

"What's going on?" Katy asked. She pushed herself up in her bed.

"I have a surprise for you today. You're skipping lessons this morning and coming with me." Her smile seemed as though it was trying to spread across her entire face. "Come down and have breakfast then we'll head out." She turned again as she reached the door. "Oh, and wear riding clothes."

"All right, I'll be right down." Katy lay back down in her bed and gazed around her room. The Queen had decorated it years ago in preparation. It still amazed her. It was a round room with a red sofa that hugged the wall under the windows. She would sit on that sofa with her feet tucked under her, watching the busy courtyard with strange creatures coming in and out, and wonder if this would ever seem normal to her. The sofa and the bed were made of a material she had never experienced, so soft to the touch it was nearly impossible to want to leave. There was a fireplace that was lit each night by a fat squat toad. He would come in every evening, do his duty, smile widely, and then hop out of the room without a word. From all over the ceiling at various heights hung the most beautiful iridescent material in deep shades of red and white that had been cut into hearts. They hung as if from invisible thread.

Her heart was full. Last night had been almost too much magic and wonder for one heart to hold. It hardly seemed real. She never imagined that a life that started such as hers, with parents who only tolerated the sight of her and "friends" who could hardly stand to be near her, could become such a beautiful fairytale. The Queen was the mother every little girl deserves. She doted and laughed and never held back affection. Being part of the royal family was so fun and full of adventure, not at all as Katy had imagined life in the English palace she had once visited. She breathed in deeply, trying to capture every moment and bottle it in her mind should she ever need it. She had known misery in her life, and she never forgot that it existed.

She dressed and trotted down to the table.

"G-g-g-good morn-n-n-ning, Miss K-K-Katy." It was Lutwidge. She had met him the first day and fallen in love with his kind spirit. He was a tall, thin lizard who worked in the palace. He was standing by the table now, with a towel draped over his arm and a chair pulled out for her. She remembered a time when she'd had a particularly long conversation with him. He had patted her hand and told her that the lovely thing about having such trouble talking was that when you found someone who was patient enough to listen, you knew that they truly were a kind soul who cared for you. She had kissed his cheek and told him she was very lucky to have met him.

Katy thanked Lutwidge and took her seat at the table. Her mother was in a very animated conversation with a small rodent similar to a weasel that was standing on the table in front of the Queen's breakfast. Eisley sat across the table spooning food into her mouth and trying to contain her smile. Katy ate her breakfast while half listening to the weasel-like creature ranting to her mother about the mome raths getting in her garden again. Katy chuckled to herself. Almost before she had a chance to set her fork down, Eisley grabbed her hand. They both kissed their mother's cheek and ran out to the courtyard.

A strongly built man with wild blond hair stood holding the reins to two beautiful mares: a dapple grey with a silver mane and tail, and a horse as black as Katy's hair, but with a streak of dark red in her mane and tail. She looked harder at the man holding the horses. He smiled, but his eyes registered nothing. She realized that this must be Degrit's father and felt a pang of compassion for him. She'd seen him many times before, but felt like she was seeing him for the first time today.

Eisley thanked him and took the reigns. She turned to Katy.

"This is the first part of my surprise." She gestured to the black and red mare. "She's yours. I have been searching the countryside for the perfect horse for you. Isn't she beautiful? She looks as though she was made for you." Indeed, Katy matched the horse perfectly. Her raven black hair was tied in a long braid that swung behind her, and the dress she had chosen was a simple deep red frock with black lace-up boots. They did seem to be made for each other. Katy walked up cautiously. She let the horse smell her hand and then stroked its silky mane.

"Eisley, she is perfect. How can I thank you?" She nuzzled her face into the horse's mane.

"No need. It's my great pleasure to gift her to you. Her name is Fleetfoot."

Katy chuckled. The events of last night kept rising to her mind. "Are you ready?" She looked over and saw Eisley seated in the saddle, anxious to head out.

Katy stepped into the stirrup and mounted the most beautiful thing she had ever owned. She stroked her mane again.

"Try and keep up!" Eisley galloped out of the courtyard, laughing.

"All right, Fleetfoot, let's see if you can live up to your name." The horse nearly shot out from under her. As though she had understood the challenge, she stayed on Eisley's heels the entire ride.

Eisley pulled back on the reigns and stopped just outside of a quaint village Katy was unfamiliar with. She hopped down and tied her horse to a tree. Katy did the same.

"Where are we?" she asked.

"This is Lewisville. And are you ready?" She paused dramatically. "This is where my match lives!! And today we are going to begin the wedding preparations." Eisley squealed, grabbed Katy's hands, and hopped up and down. Katy joined in the celebrating.

"Eisley, this is so exciting!"

"I know! I am allowed to bring one attendant or friend and I didn't even have to think who I would choose. I was desperate for you to come with me."

Katy knew that seventeen was the marrying age for the royal family. Not that they had to marry at seventeen, but they could. There were not nearly as many rules here about who you could marry as in the Shadowlands. The Queen used to say, "I want you to marry someone you love so much that it spills out and lands on anyone who gets close to you." And Katy even heard her once say, "I suppose a stable boy might just make a better king than a prince."

Katy could see that Eisley's love was already beginning to spill over. She felt quite shocked, though. She hadn't even known that Eisley was in love. She had noticed that she had been gone quite a lot from the palace lately.

Eisley squeezed her hand. "Come on! I want you to meet him!" She pulled Katy toward the tallest house in town. "This is the courter's house. We have to meet here till we are married."

The courter opened the door before they even reached the steps. Katy nearly stopped in her tracks. The courter was a tall skinny bird with fuzzy feathers and a thick heavy dress draped over her thin frame. She looked so like her mother from the Shadowlands. It was like remembering a dream from ages ago. Katy felt like a brick had landed in her stomach.

"Come, come. Mustn't linger in the doorway all day." Katy gawked at the spindly bird. "Oh yes, begging your pardon. You must be Miss Katy. I am Ms. Pinkington." Katy shook herself out of her stupor and curtsied to the bird, then stepped into the house.

* * *

Most of the day was spent with the three of them talking over wedding plans, looking at dresses, tasting different types of cake, and listening to several different singers and poets who hoped to perform at the royal wedding.

Katy felt somehow younger with the memory of her mother uncovered, as though she were eight years old again and incapable of making a decent decision or behaving as she was expected. She was sipping yet another punch flavor when there was a knock at the door. Ms. Pinkington pulled a gold watch from her pocket and tapped it. Katy caught herself wondering if it was a Pennington watch for just a moment.

"Ah, time for Mr. Thade to arrive," Ms. Pinkington squawked.

Eisley stood and walked toward the door. Ms. Pinkington opened it and there he stood. He was tall with broad shoulders and ginger hair. His eyes were brown and his nose was dotted with freckles. He looked like a man with a boy's face. Katy instantly saw why Eisley liked him. He smiled easily and laughed as he picked Eisley up in his arms and twirled her around.

"You must be Miss Katy," he said shifting his gaze toward her. "I've heard so much about you. Hair like a raven...amazing." He ran a strand of her hair between his fingers. "I'm Thaddeus." He held his hand out to her and forced a smile that Katy found difficult to believe. Katy felt uncomfortable beneath his gaze. Something about the way he looked at her made her feel naked and vulnerable.

* * *

As they rode back home at a much more leisurely pace, Eisley filled Katy in on all the details she had missed.

"Thad works as a builder. He built half of the village practically on his own. I met him when I came to help the village elect their next set of judges." She sighed deeply. "Oh, Katylove, how did we get to be so lucky?" Her eyes got glassy. "If only Daddy were here. He would be so happy."

Katy smiled. She thought again of the pocketwatch, the Shadowlands, and the only father she had known, a father that didn't match the stories and descriptions she had heard over and over since she arrived in Wonderland. The King had been loving, safe, welcoming, and full of laughter. She had once had a father, but never a father's love.

She had begun to feel a safety in Wonderland that she was thought was unshakable, until today. Too many memories of the Shadowlands, too many emotions. That look Thaddeus had given her — she had felt it before, but not in Wonderland. She was not enough, or too much, or both at the same time somehow.

Katy felt a divide. She was a puzzle piece with stark black hair that wouldn't quite fit into the picture. She'd thought at first that she had found her place in Wonderland, but now she doubted she would ever fit anywhere.

CHAPTER 7

KATY loved to be near the Queen, even if just to watch her work, which was her assignment today. Waith thought it would be good for her to begin observing some of the Queen's duties.

"Today is being a day when the Queen will hear her subjects in whatever things they have to be heard by her," Waith said. "It should be quite educational." He smiled his toothless smile.

Katy settled herself in a large red velvet chair along the side of the wall with a good view of the Queen on her throne and a good view of the line of subjects waiting to be heard. She tried to push aside her doubts after her visit with Thaddeus. She put all her energy into the present. Waith made the official announcement to the anxious crowd that the Queen was now ready to begin hearing her subjects. He gestured with his tail that the first in line should approach.

A medium-sized griffin took a few steps forward and bowed low. He began to speak. His voice was deep and full like thunder.

"Your Majesty, I am in need of your good judgment. I was recently wandering on my beach and came across a large egg. It was shaking fiercely, and I stopped to see what type of creature might emerge." He paused for a moment and glanced behind him. "I waited for a time, and as I had thought, the egg began to crack. The next thing I saw quite astounded me. I saw what appeared to be a human hand poking through the crack. I know that Your Ladyship is very busy so I shall get to the point. I am now having in my care a set of twins. Boys, bald as dolphins and none too bright. But they are in need of much care. I have been feeding and tending to them as best I could for the last week, but I am not well-suited to the task, and being the guardian of the beach, I have not the time to be their guardian as well. They get into a fair bit of mischief." He bowed low again and gestured for the tots to be brought forward. They were but a week old and were already the size of three-year-olds and tottering around on their own. They staggered up next to the griffin. One of them tugged on the griffin's wing and pointed to his open mouth. "No eating now," the griffin whispered. "Your Majesty, may I present Dee and Dum to you, and may I humbly beg for your wisdom in finding a more suitable home for them." One of the twins reached up and grabbed hold of the other's ear. The other put his finger in the first twin's nose and there they stood in a most ridiculous pose looking toward the Queen.

The Queen chuckled quietly. "Well, Mr. Griffin, first let me say that it was most kind of you to care for these boys as you have. I should like to think this matter over for a bit. If you could step to the side and wait, I will call you up again should the answer present itself." The griffin sighed with relief, bowed again, and stepped to the side. The tots waddled behind him and grabbed at his tail.

The Queen then dealt with a badger who had behaved very honorably and had rescued a young beaver who had fallen into a fissel vine, which is a vine that causes one to age so fast that if you don't get out quick, there may be nothing left of you but a skeleton. He was receiving a medal.

Then the tall bird Katy had met with Eisley, Ms. Pinkington, had some wedding business to discuss with the Queen. Katy felt the knot in her stomach again at the mention of the wedding. She stared down at her hands until Ms. Pinkington waddled off. After that, a peculiar round woman with rosy cheeks approached the throne.

"Your Ladyship," she spoke quickly and seemingly without breath. "I am quite honored to be here. I, I have need of something, although I am not altogether certain what it is that I am in need of. I feel I have come here before, but I'm not sure if that is just one of my silly imaginings. Do you know that I have thirty-seven dreams every night? Sometimes I get very confused about if I am awake or asleep. Is it quite wrong to have so many dreams? I want to do a great many things, but I just don't know how to get started. Sometimes I put on my shoes and coat to go and do one of those things, and when I am half way down the lane I wonder what I shall have for dinner, and then I find myself in the kitchen again cooking up a mince pie." Here she paused for a brief moment, and the Queen jumped in while she could.

"Ms. Tweedle. You have come here before, indeed. Nearly every week we are graced with your presence, and I think this week I have what it is that you are in need of." She looked to the chairs along the side. "Mr. Griffin, will you come forward with Dee and Dum?" The griffin herded the twins to the side of the throne. "Ms. Tweedle, I think what you have been in need of is a great purpose, and I happen to have one for you. These two lovely round boys, Dee and Dum, have hatched on the beach and are in need of someone to be their mother. Ms. Tweedle, as your Queen, I have great faith that this is exactly what you are in need of, and they are desperately in need of you. Will you accept this very great responsibility?" Ms. Tweedle didn't need a moment to think. She picked both boys up in an instant and clung to them. They seemed quite content there in her arms.

"Your Majesty, I am so very honored, and I will look after them the very best I can, and I will love them and cook for them." She bowed her head, and the Queen smiled and waved goodbye to the new family.

"Go on and introduce them to their new home," she said.

"Yes ma'am. I'll take them home straight away. Thank you, thank you." As she left the palace, Katy heard the griffin whispering the same thing to the Queen.

* * *

At dinner that night Katy was still mulling over some of the day's proceedings.

"Mother, how do you know that Ms. Tweedle will be a good mother for those boys? She seems quite mad."

The Queen laughed. "Ms. Tweedle is a good woman. She's not mad, just lonely and bored. I suspect this arrangement is just the one they all need. Sometimes making wise decisions is just a matter of following your heart. And, Katylove, that is something you are very good at indeed." The Queen patted her hand. "Just beware, my dear, a heart is a very passionate thing, and if you don't take care of it and learn to love it, you won't be able to love anyone else's, and that could lead to terrible things."

CHAPTER 8

It had been weeks since Katy had even seen a hint of Degrit. Each time she wandered the land with Waith, she would keep a close eye out for any sign of movement. She felt as though she may have imagined that magical night. Did fleets even exist? Had she really shared those lights and those words with that wild-haired boy?

She was determined to find out for herself. She longed to see the colors and lights again. The castle was dark, all the inhabitants long since sleeping. The ground felt cold even through her shoes as she headed into the forest. The air was strange tonight, as though it were vibrating. For a moment, Katy thought of running back into the castle to the safety of her room and those floating hearts, but her determination was stronger than her fear.

She was nearing the meadow and starting to feel a bit more at ease when she heard something rustling in the trees. It surely must be Degrit. She jumped toward the sound to catch him. She landed right in front of a creature she had never seen and Waith had never warned her about. He was shaped a bit like a greyhound she had seen once in the Shadowlands. He had stripes racing from his nose to his tail in blacks and greys. His teeth were as sharp as blades and glistening with drool. She was most disturbed by his eyes. They glowed a deep red and grew even brighter when he spotted her. Two pups were hiding behind his thin back legs. Katy began to back away with her hands in front of her in a sincere sign of surrender.

"I'm so very sorry," she began. "I thought you were someone else." The creature came closer and began to make a deep sound, more of a vibration than a growl as he approached. She was making a plan to turn and run, although feeling very uncertain considering the build of this animal. Surely it would be able to outrun her. She backed through the woods and spun around to flee, but there in front of her were two more of the creatures, their eyes glowing menacingly. Katy began to cry and realized this may well be the end. She mustered the courage to at least attempt to save herself.

There was an opening to her right toward the palace. She bolted suddenly as fast as she could. She ran faster than she ever had. Her lungs burned and tears streaked toward her ears. She could hear the creatures behind her, gaining on her. She looked back and saw red eyes — how many she couldn't be sure. She turned on as much speed as she could, but alas, her lack of vision was her downfall. In the darkness she couldn't see a rather large tree branch hanging at such a low height as to strike her just across the face. By the time she spotted it there was no way to avoid it.

The next thing she remembered was fire and a loud shout. Green eyes. Blond hair. Trees overhead.

* * *

Katy woke up in her bed with her mother sitting beside her, dabbing her face with a damp cloth. She was disoriented and confused.

"What happened?" she asked. Her mother's eyes teared up as she heard Katy speak.

"Oh, dearest, thank goodness you're all right. The healer was unsure." She sighed deeply. "You were attacked by billdralls," she said.

"Billdralls?" Katy asked.

"They only come out twice a year. The rest of the time they live underground. They come out to breed and to introduce their young. Those are very dangerous nights to be out. Could you feel the vibrations?" Katy furrowed her brow and thought hard.

"Um...I remember putting on my coat....yes. Yes. I do remember the vibrations. I almost ran home when I felt them." It was painful to talk and she winced from the effort.

"If you are ever out at night and feel them again, you must run home immediately. Do you understand?"

Katy nodded. "I'm so sorry, mother. I shouldn't have gone out on my own." She tried to sit up, but found herself too weak. "How did I escape? I remember running, but I don't remember much after that."

"Thankfully, Degrit practically lives in the forest. He was staying high in the trees last night. He could feel that it was a night that the billdralls would be out. He heard them giving chase and ran through the tops of the trees to see what was going on. He saw you just as you hit the tree. He was in a flame tree." Katy had learned about flame trees from Waith. The wood from a flame tree would catch fire when you hit it hard with another flame stick. "He jumped down from the trees with flame sticks lit and scared off all the billdralls. Then he carried you home. We begged him to stay and eat and rest, but he rushed off. We shall forever be in his debt."

"Yes," Katy agreed.

"Tell me, Katylove, what is it you were doing in the forest at night?"

"I was looking for fleets," she said.

The Queen laughed a loud laugh full of relief and exhaustion. "Oh my dear, we shall fill the palace with fleets if that is what you wish. Just please don't put your life in danger again to search for insects. Just tell me what you desire next time and I shall arrange it for you."

"Mother? What would you think about Degrit teaching me about the forest?" she asked. "I was just thinking that Degrit knows more about the forest than anyone. And...well...maybe he could take over my outdoor studies. He can teach me all I need to know. And Waith could still teach me all of the things I need to learn in the palace."

"I think that is a fine idea," the Queen said. "We shall discuss it with Waith and Degrit right away."

CHAPTER 9

KATY'S recovery was slow, and she stayed in the castle for the first
couple weeks. Her face was swollen and scratched, and it was painful to
chew or talk. Waith hardly left her side. He filled her room with jars of
fleets. It reminded her of Christmas in the Shadowlands, all the
twinkling lights. He felt responsible for her injury, having never taught
her the dangers of billdralls. She assured him repeatedly that it was her
own fault for being stupid enough to venture out of the palace on her
own at night.

At last her face began to take on its normal shape again, and her
energy started to return. By the third week she spent some of her time
in the courtyard watching the comings and goings of all the strange
and wonderful creatures. She didn't feel as brave as she once had.

Eisley convinced her to take a short journey with her to visit
Thaddeus. She mounted Fleetfoot and stayed close beside Eisley. She
felt vulnerable and unsure. The ordeal with the billdralls had stolen
much of her courage, and being around Thaddeus made her keenly
aware of all her flaws. Eisley was so easy to be around, though. She
quickly helped Katy laugh and relax a bit. The journey wasn't far, but

Katy felt exhausted from the ride. They tied up their horses and headed toward Ms. Pinkington's house.

Eisley held Katy's hand, for which Katy was very thankful. She felt silly for being so afraid. It was nice to be with Eisley, who seemed to know what she was thinking.

Ms. Pinkington met them at the door with her usually fussiness. "Well, come on in. No use lingering on the doorstep. Come in, come in." Katy followed Eisley and they settled on a deep billowy couch. Katy leaned into Eisley. Ms. Pinkington ran to notify Thaddeus that they had arrived.

"Oh, Katylove, you're going to be all right. This too shall pass, my darling," Eisley said, patting her hand.

"I know," she sighed. "I just hate feeling so afraid all the time."

"Your courage will find itself again. Soon enough." She smiled at Katy then kissed her on the cheek.

The door swung open and Thaddeus bounded in. He filled up the room with his laugh and his smile. He picked up Eisley and hugged her. He kissed Katy gently on the hand, keeping his eyes on Eisley.

"It's good to see you out and about, Katy. This country air will do you good." His voice was flat when he spoke to her. Katy smiled and nodded. Ms. Pinkington appeared at her shoulder with a cup of tea and a biscuit.

"Thank you, Ms. Pinkington," she said.

"Of course, dear. We are all very glad that you're doing better." Katy realized that Ms. Pinkington had much more compassion than her bird-mother from the Shadowlands. She nearly laughed aloud at the thought that a bird was a better comforter than a human mother.

She sat sipping her tea and watching Eisley and Thaddeus, who sat in the courtyard on a swing made for two. They looked so

43

happy...laughing, fingers intertwined, whispering to each other. She was enchanted by their love, then for a moment Thaddeus' eyes cut to the side and there was a flash of something terrifying. It was gone so fast that she wondered if she had even seen it. She assured herself that it had been her imagination. She was in such a fearful state that it must be causing her to see things that aren't really there.

After enjoying a nice long lunch with Thaddeus and Ms. Pinkington, Eisley and Katy mounted their horses and began the journey home. They took their time.

"I don't think Thaddeus likes me much," Katy said. Eisley looked at her with surprise.

"Of course he does. Don't be silly." She looked back toward the trail again. "You just don't know each other very well yet. He loves you. You are to be his sister soon." She reached over and patted Katy's hand. "You are just in a bad state of mind right now. The billdralls shook your confidence, and it makes the whole world seem wrong. You'll be right as rain soon enough."

Katy hoped she was right.

CHAPTER 10

KATY sat at breakfast moving her eggs around on her plate when Lutwidge came in with a large bouquet of flowers.

"M-m-miss K-Katy, these are f-f-for you." He smiled. "I thought I sh-should g-g-give them t-to you when you c-c-could enjoy them. T-t-that's why I w-w-waited until you were b-b-better to g-g-give them to you."

"How very clever of you, Lutwidge. Thank you so much. They are beautiful." He bowed and left the room.

"He is such a kind creature," Eisley said, bending over and smelling the flowers.

"Yes, he is so dear," Katy agreed.

The door opened again and Lutwidge entered.

"M-m-miss K-katy, there is a D-D-Degrit here t-t-to see you." Katy stood and thanked Lutwidge.

She walked out into the foyer where Degrit was waiting in long pants, shoes, and a shirt.

"You're dressed," Katy observed. He looked down and admired his obviously new clothes.

"Well, the Queen insisted on getting me new clothes and paying me a fair sum. I told her she needn't pay me, but she insisted."

"Well, I'm very glad she did. And I'm glad you agreed to this arrangement. I thought maybe you would say 'no.'" He blushed and shook his head. "By the way, thank you. For saving my life."

"I'm just glad I was there. I didn't know if you would make it. When I got you to the palace your face was nothing but blood. I worried that I had been too late."

"I'm much better now, thanks to you." He shifted nervously at her praise. "Tell me. What is our lesson to be today, oh great teacher?"

"I prefer it if you call me lord," he said with a grin.

"Oh, but of course," she laughed.

* * *

As they strolled slowly through the woods together they discussed all the things Waith had covered with her and all the things he hadn't. They hadn't yet talked about any night creatures. But, she didn't feel ready for that education quite yet. Her last experience had left her shaken. She felt safe with Degrit and she knew that he understood the forest better than anyone. She had often wondered what Waith would do if they were attacked. She loved him dearly but didn't find much safety in a toothless serpent.

Degrit suggested a spot near his village to begin. As they approached the village of Wootenton, Degrit pointed out landmarks that represented important moments from his childhood, like the Crane's house where he'd gotten his first haircut. Katy now thought she understood why his hair was so wild — a crane doesn't even have hands to hold scissors. When Katy mentioned this Degrit laughed and explained that he snips it with his beak.

In the center of town they stopped at a crooked little building which had been Degrit's school. He laughed telling her all the torment he had put his teacher through. She liked his laugh. It was pure, even when it was in relation to torturing tutors. Katy felt her fears began to melt away in his presence. She asked why he no longer attended school. He grew quiet and said things changed when his mother died.

There was a large family of rabbits that lived near the outskirts of town. Katy had never seen so many rabbits. They were surrounding a little pink house; hanging out the wash, beating rugs, stirring a large pot over a fire. Tiny bunnies were everywhere. Most of the little ones were playing games that involved hopping contests or skipping rope.

"This family is mine. They took me in when my mother died. My father went on a long journey just after, and I was alone. Mrs. Warren, their mother, came to my house and brought me here. She wouldn't take no for an answer, and for several months this was my home." He smiled at all the activity around him. "I love these rabbits very much. They all accepted me as one of them. I became quite good at jumping while I stayed here. I'm not as good as they are, of course, but for a non-rabbit I was quite good."

Katy smiled at him. "I'd like to see that sometime," she said.

"All right, how about now?" He grabbed her hand and they jumped into a skipping rope. Katy had to jump out after just a moment. The rope got higher and higher with each swing until Degrit's knees seemed to be coming nearly to his ears. When he jumped out, he was breathing heavily, and all the little bunnies were cheering. He gave them hugs and kissed the little girl bunnies on the head.

"This is my friend, Katy," he said. They all rushed her and clambered over each other trying to shake her hand or touch her hair.

She watched Degrit laughing and then saw a medium sized greyish rabbit approach him. They embraced. She could see they must be close in age and they were very much dear to each other. Degrit spoke to him for a few moments while Katy passed out some sweets she had hidden in her pocket. The small ones went off giggling and sucking on hard candies.

"Katy, I would like you to meet my dearest friend, Nash." Degrit stood with the grey rabbit at his side. Katy shook his hand and smiled.

"It's so nice to meet you," she said.

"A pleasure," Nash said. He fidgeted with his coat. "I'm glad that you are spending time with Degrit for him to teach you. He has great knowledge of the things you need learning and he is a good teacher. Now maybe my mother won't worry about him so much!"

Katy smiled. She felt comfortable with this family. She suspected that they had a way of making anyone feel at home among them.

"Oh, you must come for dinner," he added. "After your lesson, come by for an early dinner before you head back to the palace. My mother would love to cook for you."

"That's very kind. We would be honored," Katy responded.

Degrit clapped his hands together, then rubbed them excitedly. "Katy, are you ready for class? I can't wait to show you today's lesson. You're going to love it." He waved to the rabbits and headed toward the forest.

CHAPTER 11

KATY ran to catch up with Degrit.

"Just where are we going, and what will we be seeing?" Katy asked. Degrit was bent over, breaking sticks apart and laying them against a nearby tree.

"Well, we're nearly there. But first, you must eat a bit of this." He measured out a bit of cake that he had wrapped in a handkerchief and put into his pocket before they set out. "That should be about the right amount." Moments after swallowing, she noticed the ground coming up to greet her and realized that she was indeed shrinking. (She had become quite used to changing size since first arriving. She had mastered the mushrooms in the library within the first week. She found it great fun changing heights to reach books.)

In a moment Degrit had shrunk down to meet her.

"Perfect," he said. "Now, before we go any further, I want you to know that I won't let anything happen to you. I need you to trust me." He looked at her intently.

She nodded. "I do," she said.

"All right, we are going underground, and we're going to take these flame sticks with us." He picked up the sticks he had set against the tree moments ago and smacked them together. They caught flame and lit up his excited expression.

He started down a large hole hidden behind a boulder. Katy followed close behind, clutching her flame stick torch. She smelled something familiar and began to feel a little unsettled, but she trusted Degrit and knew he wouldn't take her into harm's way.

They walked for ten or fifteen minutes in a cool damp tunnel before it suddenly opened up into a vast room. It was full of barking type sounds and some others she was not familiar with. She squinted her eyes and saw puppies bounding around and playfully tugging at each other's ears. She had a sudden realization; these were not just any pups. The glowing red eyes...Degrit had brought her to the billdralls! She stepped closer to Degrit and clutched his hand. He looked over at her. She was shaking. He put his arm around her shoulders and pulled her close.

"It's all right. Just watch. I wanted you to see that they're really very gentle and kind. They're only dangerous twice a year, and if you never venture down below to see them then you'll always believe that they are nothing but monsters. And that could not be further from the truth. Sometimes you have to go out of your way to know someone, but usually if you look hard enough you will find something lovable in them."

"Do they know we are here?" she whispered.

"Oh, yes. They have an excellent sense of smell. Their hearing is also superb. And they can see in the dark," he said. Katy wanted to run, to escape. She wondered why she had trusted Degrit so absolutely. He must be crazy dragging her down to a den of wild dogs that had nearly killed her just a few weeks before. She knew there was no way out. She had seen their speed before and at the size she was now she would barely even turn around before she would be caught. She felt panic starting to grip her but Degrit seemed so sure of himself that she dug up courage enough to just stand and watch.

As she did, she began to see what Degrit meant. She watched two pups playing tug-of-war with an old piece of rope. Another pup that watched from the sidelines would wait till one had the upper hand, then charge in and bite that pup on the tail, and a massive puppy brawl would ensue. This happened repeatedly, and his mother, who was stretched out in an area where most of the adults were lounging, would sigh, stand up, and drag him off to another area only to have to do it all over again in moments. Katy laughed aloud the fourth time this happened. A few times, a pup brushed against her leg, and an adult even walked past them without concern. She was entranced and didn't realize that time hadn't stopped.

"Come on, I still have something else to show you." Degrit gestured toward the way out. She nodded and followed, still holding tight to his hand.

When they reached the topside, she breathed a deep breath of the fresh, woodsy air. They put out their flame sticks and sat in the grass for a moment.

"Well, what did you think?" Degrit asked.

"I hardly know what to think. I've never felt terrified and delighted at nearly the same time. It's like being forced to drink what you think is poison and finding that it's really quite good for you," she said.

He smiled. "Sometimes when I am feeling hopeless about things I will go down and watch the billdralls. Being with them in that cool and dark place, smelling the earth, watching puppies playing, and watching a family..." He trailed off. "It does seem to be good medicine for the soul."

Katy nodded. "I was so upset by what happened to you, but I wanted you to know that there is more to their story. And more to yours."

"Thank you," she said. "I would never have believed that there was any goodness in them unless I had seen it myself."

"And now, we must hurry on. Mrs. Warren always has dinner on by six." He grabbed her hand and pulled her up. "We still have one more spot to visit before we head back. I think you will like this place very much."

CHAPTER 12

DEGRIT handed Katy another piece of cake. After they had eaten it and grown again to their proper height, they headed toward Degrit's next lesson. Katy was still reeling from the last experience. They walked along in silence, leaving each other to their thoughts.

The sun became dimmer and the sound of running water could be heard through the trees. As they crossed through the last bit of brush, their destination became apparent. There was a clearing where the sunlight filtered in, and a beautiful stream raced across the face of the land.

"This is the Babbling Brook," said Degrit. "It's a quiet place. You sit on the banks and put your bare feet in and then you listen. You must be quiet to hear her." He gestured for Katy to do so. She sat on the banks and unlaced her boots. The water felt icy as she slid her feet in. It sounded like any other stream, but she sat patiently, waiting and listening. When she was nearly asleep, lying on the bank with her feet dangling in the icy stream, she heard something like whispers. She sat up on her elbows and concentrated harder. A faint whisper came more and more into focus almost like a blurry image. The voice was like a woman's, but not human.

"A tender heart...a raven with feathers of satin...speaking words that bring comfort." There was a long pause and only the sound of water. "Strong in love...vulnerable in pain. Guard your heart. Hold to who you know yourself to be right now." There was a loud sound like water sighing.

Degrit touched her shoulder. "That sound means she's finished speaking for now."

She had nearly forgotten that anyone was there with her. She breathed in at the surprise.

"Sorry, I didn't mean to startle you. You're very lucky, you know. Sometimes she speaks truth or insight like she just did, but most of the time she babbles nonsense. Last time I came, she told me bats should be underwater creatures because their wings are much better suited for swimming."

Katy laughed and took his hand as he helped her up. "Has she ever spoken to you like that?" she asked.

"Yes, twice, and the words are in the forever part of my mind. Once just after my mother died, and then again just after I met you. I come here a lot, because even when you don't hear something that matters, just being here, being quiet and still, does something good for your soul."

"Yes, I can see what you mean. It's a very peaceful place, but I don't think I understand what she meant when she spoke to me."

"You're not always meant to. Sometimes the words are for this moment, sometimes they're for a past hurt, and sometimes they're for a future moment. You must save them in small jars in your heart until the day you know you need them."

Katy hoped the words would not ever leave her. They were beautiful even though she had no idea what they really meant. Someday, maybe, they would click into place like that last missing puzzle piece.

* * *

When they arrived at the Warrens' cozy little pink house they were greeted at the front gate by several small bunnies.

"Come in, come in. We're all ready for you!" They hopped around excitedly as they led them through the doorway and into a long, narrow room. The floor was covered with a long blanket that was crowded with food. Rabbits of all shapes and sizes were seated on either side of the blanket, all along the walls of the room. There were even a few non-rabbits. Katy noticed a small bluebird and two hedgehogs among the crowd.

All were chattering excitedly as the little ones led Katy and Degrit to two small cushions near Nash. He smiled over at them, and the room fell silent as a large grey rabbit walked into the room.

"That's Mr. Warren," Degrit whispered. The family watched him in awe as he entered the room and arranged himself on a large cushion at the end of the blanket. Katy could see a smile starting at the corner of his mouth. Then all at once a wide smile erupted across his face, and he spread his arms toward the food.

"Shall we eat?" he asked. The children all hopped and giggled in their seats. The older siblings stood and began to serve the younger ones. There were several large pots of what appeared to be carrot stew, surrounded by loaves of brown bread, plates of berries, and jugs of fresh milk. Katy enjoyed the food, but more than that she enjoyed watching the family laugh together.

"How many children do they have?" Katy whispered to Degrit.

"They have seventeen, but they take in any animal that needs a family. So the number is constantly changing." Katy thought it was strange how a family so large could feel so small. No creature could feel lonely or overlooked in this clan.

After dinner they sat laughing and telling stories of adventures they had shared. Katy and Degrit thanked them for the lovely dinner, and Nash walked them to the edge of the village. He was a quiet and kind rabbit, but nervous and fidgety. Degrit later said that he was nervous to meet a real princess. Katy laughed. She may be a princess in role, but she felt like an ordinary girl in every other way, a very lucky ordinary girl. She remembered her past life and thought that things could have been very, very different.

CHAPTER 13

FOR the next several days Katy was very busy at the palace. Waith wanted her to be in court for several important cases. He thought it was a necessary learning experience. She willingly did as Waith asked. She was very fond of him and always considered him to be like an older brother to her.

Then Ms. Pinkington got a hold of her. There were fittings and consultations in preparation for the upcoming wedding. The entire kingdom was preparing for the celebration. Katy was notified that she would be singing a traditional song at the wedding. When she protested that she couldn't sing Ms. Pinkington wouldn't hear it. Her mother was a much more sympathetic ear. She suggested that instead, Katy read it like a poem. Katy was very relieved.

While she enjoyed all the goings-on at the palace and the busyness of the wedding, she was anxious to be with Degrit again. She'd never had a friend like him before, and she found herself wanting to spend more and more time with him. He helped her see everything with new eyes.

At last she had a free day, and she nearly bowled Degrit over running out of the castle to find him. They both had a good laugh.

"Degrit, I'm so sorry. I was running to find you!" She stopped to catch her breath.

"Waith found me this morning and told me that you would perhaps be ready for another lesson." He eyed a package she clutched in her hand.

"I have a lesson for you too," she said.

"Oh, I see." He raised an eyebrow.

They headed toward an area known as The Garden. Degrit started talking as they crossed the Vast Meadowlands.

"Waith said that he told you about some of the flowers in The Garden, but not all of them. Have you been here before?"

She looked down at her feet. "Waith told me not to. He found me playing with a school of snawlish one day before I knew they were dangerous, and he had to pull me to safety. After that he was very cautious with me and very stern. I really was careful to do what he said until the night I snuck out to find the fleets again." She looked up at him. "I was really looking for you."

"You found me," he said. She laughed. He continued, "I think you're going to like The Garden very much, but you must stay near me. A few of the flowers are very dangerous. Some of them speak and some do not, but they're not really all that friendly to nonflowers. There is also a vine called fissel vine, and if your skin touches it you will age so fast you may die before you get out."

"Yes, I've heard about it. I was in with the Queen one day and a badger was receiving a medal for rescuing someone from it," she said.

"It's bright green with small red flowers, and it smells delicious. Just don't get near it no matter how tempting it smells. Stay near me and you'll be fine," he said.

Katy fidgeted as they walked. She was more aware of all her flaws since meeting Thaddeus: her short stubby fingers, her inability to keep her mouth shut. Even her raven hair brought on bouts of desperate insecurity. A fear had taken root in her heart, one that was not unfamiliar to her. It had been her constant companion in the Shadowlands. Being with Degrit was just the medicine she needed.

The Garden was indeed breathtaking. Katy had never seen anything like it. It was full of warm fragrances, and the sunlight seemed to dance on the petals. Some of the flowers were very like ones that she had seen near the palace or in the Shadowlands. Some were totally foreign to her. She could hear murmuring amongst the plants, but tried to ignore it. There was one flower in particular that intrigued her. She had seen it before at the palace. It had a tall dark green stalk and the petals were silver and blue. It looked as though it were chiseled from metal and stone. It was so regal and beautiful, but somehow so cold.

"Ah, the sterling, it's nicknamed the 'royal flower.' It's the flower used in all royal celebrations. Beautiful, but without fragrance. It's very strong. Even when picked it lives and thrives for months," Degrit said.

She touched the petals and was surprised to find that they were hard, just like the metal they resembled.

"It's not my favorite," Degrit said. "I think there is something beautiful about a flower that is more delicate and vulnerable. Here." He led her to a flower that was pure white with a splash of dark red among the center petals. The stalk was black as night. "Smell it," he said. She inhaled deeply. It smelled of cinnamon, sandalwood, and clove. "It only lives for a few days, and if you pick it, it only lasts hours before it wilts. She's my favorite. She's called a reedia."

"She's beautiful and smells...delicious." There was a loud chorus of giggling behind them. She twirled around to see a bed of daisies laughing and pointing at them with their leaves. Degrit took her arm.

59

"Come on. It's no use trying to converse with them. They are only interested in berating others." They followed the path through the garden. "There," he said, pointing, "that is fissel vine. You can even smell it from here. If you ever smell that again, then you know to watch for it." She nodded. The smell was a unique mix of floral and sweet and she didn't think she would soon forget it.

At that moment, a small woodchuck hopped up on the path and struck up a conversation with Degrit. They had apparently known each other for quite some time. The little woodchuck had found a wife and had a family since last they had met. There was quite a lot of catching up that needed to happen.

Katy noticed a patch of purple and gold flowers that were growing at the bottom of a large flame tree. They were tall and trumpet-like. She left Degrit to his chatting and walked over to get a closer look.

She inhaled deeply as she got closer and felt a sense of euphoria spreading through her body. Her fingertips, toes, and even the top of her head were tingling. She closed her eyes and suddenly she was back in the Shadowlands being embraced by Ms. Glass. She could smell the musty smells of her old house and feel Ms. Glass' arms pulling her tighter. Her head shook and her eyes flew open. She looked around. She was still in the garden. She hadn't gone anywhere. She had never felt emotion so thick and delicious and had never had a memory so vivid. She could almost still hear Ms. Glass breathing. Her eyes closed again, and this time she was laughing and riding with her mother and Eisley. The wind blew through her hair, and she felt Eisley's hand on her arm as she rode next to her. Her eyes opened again. She turned and saw the woodchuck heading back into the forest. Her head felt light. Her eyes fell shut again, and now she was in the forest with Degrit. The fleets were hovering all around the meadow. Degrit yelled and ran through them, creating a beautiful light show, then sat next to her in the grass telling her his story.

She felt a hand on the small of her back and spun around suddenly, opening her eyes. Degrit's face was inches from hers. She felt so much for him. Her heart beat faster in her chest. She leaned in and kissed him. Her arms reached up around his shoulders and pulled him closer. His arms tightened around her back. He squeezed her against him. She could feel his warmth. Then suddenly he stepped back and gently pushed her away. She looked into his eyes, confused and embarrassed.

"I'm sorry," he said, "I need to talk to you, but first we need to get away from these flowers." He took her hand and led her to a bench a good distance away. They sat down and he held her hand in both of his. She felt a churning of emotions below her skin. She didn't understand his rejection. She fought to hold back tears.

"That is the danglia, one of our most alluring flowers. It's safe in small doses, but many people have gone mad from that flower. Its fragrance is toxic and causes eventual insanity. I've seen creatures who've lost someone they love...they come to the flowers just to relive a moment with their dear one, but one moment is almost never enough when you have lost someone who's a part of you. So they come again and again and again. After a time, the sane parts of them become the minority, and they usually spend the rest of their lives speaking complete nonsense." He paused and sighed. "It is such a beautiful feeling to get lost in good memories and all the euphoria that the flower brings. It's something you must experience for yourself. I watched you from the path, and I didn't want to stop you because your face was so beautiful with the memories." She felt tears running down her cheeks. He wiped her face with his thumbs. "When you kissed me, I...I thought you were just intoxicated from the flower. I didn't know if...I didn't stop you for any reason except that I wanted it to be real. I didn't want you to regret that moment later....I..." he stumbled. Then sighed, "Katy, I, I'm..."

"It's all right," she interrupted. "I think I understand. I'm sorry. I guess I just got carried away in the moment." She stood up and began walking briskly down the path, tears falling faster. She was still slightly disoriented, but she felt certain that this was his way of letting her down easy. Degrit sat stunned for a moment, then shook his head and ran after her.

"No, no...I don't think you do understand," he said. He caught her and took both her hands again. "Do you want to know what the Brook said to me the night I met you, the night of the fleets?" She wiped the tears from her face and shrugged. "She said 'the raven is your love; take care of her' and, Katy, she was right."

Katy looked intently into his green eyes. "What do you mean?" she asked. Her mind was struggling to function properly with all the emotion swimming around in her body.

"That kiss, whether real or not, has given me enough hope and courage to say what I need to say to you now." He took a deep breath and let it out slowly. "Katy, I'm in love with you. I love you."

Her eyes widened and she stepped back. After a moment she spoke softly. "You do?" He nodded. "But I thought that...I thought that you were pushing me away."

"Just because I needed to know that you really felt the same way and it wasn't just the flowers making you crazy."

"I do," she whispered. "I do feel the same way." She hadn't realized that her heart had an empty space in it before, but it felt really full for the first time. Degrit touched her face and pulled her into a tight embrace. Time passed for the rest of Wonderland, but Degrit and Katy stayed locked in that embrace until the sun shifted its position in the sky and the flowers turned their heads toward them to follow the light.

CHAPTER 14

KATY and Degrit walked hand in hand across the Vast Meadowlands.

"Degrit, did your father ever go to the danglias after your mom died?" Katy asked.

Degrit looked ahead. "He did quite often at first. That was when I stayed with the Warrens. He would disappear for days, seeking to relive moments of happiness with Mother. I watched him steadily decline, and my pleading didn't help. In the end, Mr. Warren was the one who helped him break free of the danglia's power. He told him he was going to lose all that was important: his job at the palace, his home, his son. It was too late in some ways. He had already lost most of his love for me at that point, but at least he didn't drive himself into complete madness." He squeezed her hand.

"What about you? Did you ever go?" she asked.

He sniffed and rubbed his face with his free hand. "Nash and I snuck out once so that I could go. The memories and the feelings that I experienced there were so beautiful and perfect that I cried for days after. It was so hard to come back to reality that I never wanted to go again. Nash was so worried about me. He thought that I had gone mad from one sniff." He laughed at the memory. "When we came home he immediately confessed what we'd done to his parents. Some partner-in-crime he turned out to be! Actually, I was quite grateful for him. He stayed with me nearly every moment for weeks until I was back to myself again." He looked down at the package Katy still clutched in her hand. "So, what's in the package?" Katy matched his gaze.

"Oh, I nearly forgot. Let's find a nice flat spot and I'll show you." They found the perfect spot and sat down in the soft grass. She smoothed her dress around her and opened the little flat wooden box. Degrit was intrigued. She pulled out the cards and handed the deck to him.

"These are playing cards. Have you ever seen any before?"

He turned them over in his hands and dropped most of them. He fumbled to pick them up.

"I'm sorry," he said still struggling to get them all back in his hands. "I've never seen anything like this. They're slick. What are they...I mean what are they used for?" he asked.

She helped him get the cards into one pile.

"They're for playing games. There are lots of different games you can play with them." She watched him sorting through the cards with wonder. "But maybe today I can just introduce you to all the cards."

He was like a child seeing a new toy for the first time. She picked up the deck and spread them out face up on the lawn. "There are four different suits: spades, diamonds, clubs, and hearts." She pointed to each one in turn. "The aces are like ones." She pointed to all the aces individually. "Then the cards go from two up to ten. After ten comes the royal family. The Jack, the Queen, and the King." He picked up the Queen of Hearts and held it up, comparing it with Katy.

"It's you," he said in surprise. Katy had realized long ago that the reason people in Wonderland were so transfixed by her hair was that no other humans in this world had black hair. They had blond, red, brown...some even had blue or green, but never black. The Queen of Hearts was probably the first person other than Katy that Degrit had seen with black hair.

"Me?" she asked.

"Yes. Raven hair, white skin, a queen. And she is surrounded by hearts because she is loved and full of compassion. It's you, although she's not as beautiful as you." Katy blushed and looked down at the card. She ran her thumb along the edge of it and smiled. Degrit touched her arm. "Is it not meant to be you?"

Katy laughed. "No...in the Shadowlands many people have these cards and I was a nobody there. My parents didn't like me much. I was certainly not a queen. And lots of people there have black hair. It's just a card, not me."

He put his hand to her face.

"I'm so glad that you came to us when you did. Now you have the family you deserve. I can't imagine our kingdom without you. Someday you'll sit on your throne, and I will forever think of you as the Queen of Hearts." He leaned in and kissed her lightly on the cheek. "I cannot imagine my life without you." He tilted his head toward her. "Were you afraid when you first arrived? I watched you from the forest and you seemed so at ease...like you expected all of this," he said.

"I wasn't afraid. My last home was not a place I was sorry to leave. I read a lot of books in the Shadowlands, and my favorites were stories of people crossing over into other worlds. As soon as I saw Waith and heard him speak, I knew that's what must have happened," she said. "Either that or I had hit my head harder than I thought."

"Tell me about the Shadowlands. What is it like?" he asked.

"It is not nearly as colorful. The animals don't speak, nor do the plants or bodies of water for that matter. Only the people speak. Some people are very kind and live quite happy lives, but many are not, and there is much unhappiness. The people there are very concerned about what others think, and they live their lives based on other people's opinions. It's dark." She waved her hand back and forth across the soft grass. "Everything here is so full of wonder. I forgot to even miss home. In fact, I was glad to be free of it. I was a nuisance to my parents in many ways, and I had no friends. There was only one person I really loved back home, and she was my nanny who took care of me. I saw her again when I smelled the danglia."

"Then she must be a good memory," Degrit said.

"Her name was Ms. Glass. She truly loved me and tried to protect me from my selfish parents. But her memory faded after I met my real mother and Eisley. I always thought happiness like that was only written about in books. I never dreamed I would experience it myself." Degrit was lying on the grass staring up at her. "When you took me to see the fleets that night, I felt like I might explode with joy. For that's when I really realized that this was indeed my life and the Shadowlands had become more like a dream I hardly remembered." She looked down at him. "I wanted to see you again, but you vanished for weeks! I started to think maybe I had imagined it all."

He laughed. "I was in the forest. I was a little bit afraid after visiting the Brook. I knew I had strong feelings for you, but I didn't believe that you would ever think of me that way. So I was hiding. Then when you jumped into a pack of billdralls I decided I'd better come out of hiding."

"I'm glad you did. I almost became dog food that night," she said.

"If I'd acted a tad faster, I might have saved you from that vicious tree too," he said.

She laughed and threw a handful of grass at him.

"My face still hurts when I think about that," she said.

"You know...before I knew you...when I had just seen you coming through the woods with Waith...it took a long time to work up the nerve to talk to you. That night I saw you in the woods by yourself and I knew the fleets would be out. I just jumped at the chance while I could. I couldn't take my eyes off you that night. You were so full of awe and it was like I was seeing the fleets for the first time again."

"That was a night I'll never forget. Not just because of the fleets, but the way you spoke to me. I'd never experienced that much honesty and openness from anyone, except Eisley and Mother. I didn't know that friends could speak that way," she said.

"I couldn't help it. I wanted to tell you everything. And I did tell you almost everything."

"Almost?" Katy asked.

"Well...I didn't tell you that you were the most beautiful thing I'd ever seen. That I couldn't stop thinking about you. That I followed you and Waith on most of your lessons and watched from the trees." He chuckled to himself. "Probably a good thing. You might have tried to reassemble that shattered mirror and get back to the Shadowlands."

"It's good to hear now." She smiled at him and took his hand. "Do you still think I'm beautiful?"

"More than ever," he said.

CHAPTER 15

A cold wind blew over the courtyard, and the first few snowflakes of the year began to fall. Katy loved the winter. She had once mentioned that she missed Christmas. The Queen made a proclamation the next day that Wonderland should now celebrate Christmas, too. So they started a committee whose sole purpose was to educate the kingdom about Christmas. Katy told them everything she could think of: stockings, Christmas trees, wreaths, carols, nativities, mulling spices, pumpkin pie, presents, decorating the houses, turkey dinner. That first Christmas was a bit awkward as they all got the hang of it. But now that they had celebrated it a few years, it was as if they always had.

Eisley's wedding was to be a winter wedding and was just a few weeks away. She would be married three weeks before Christmas. Eisley had fallen in love with Christmas the moment Katy introduced it and dreamed of having a wedding with Christmas decorations and snow. Ms. Pinkington was nearly always at the palace these days as preparations got into full swing.

Katy escaped the madness as often as she could, but sadly that wasn't as often as she would have liked. Being the sister of the bride, she had many responsibilities in the wedding. Today was yet another rehearsal for the event. It was to be an outdoor winter wedding, something that Katy could never imagine happening in the Shadowlands.

There were workers all around the courtyard and the palace, hanging decorations, setting up trees, and stringing lights. This rehearsal was a walk-through for anyone who was performing at the ceremony. The bride and groom and the Queen were exempt from attending. Katy stood near the front, smoothing a worn piece of paper in her hands. It had the words to the song she would be reciting. She had memorized them but felt some comfort having them there in her hands. She pulled her scarf tighter around her neck.

Ms. Pinkington came into the courtyard, clapping her wings together and shouting to all within earshot. "All right ladies and gentlemen. It's time to get this show moving. Gather 'round and listen closely to my instructions. Now first off, here is the order of the ceremony; pay close attention to when you will be performing...." she said.

Katy tuned her out. She knew that she was to say her part as the bride walked down the aisle. She had gone over and over it in her mind. She looked around at all the participants, and as her eyes swung back to the front of the courtyard, she saw Degrit. He was walking up the center aisle, smiling slyly at her. She felt her entire being relax as he walked toward her. He hugged her and then quickly pretended to be listening to Ms. Pinkington.

"What are you doing here?" Katy whispered.

"I am performing," he said. This was the first Katy had heard about this and she was taken aback.

"What do you mean, performing?"

"You'll see," he answered. He gave her a sideways glance and that smile returned.

Ms. Pinkington was clapping her wings together again. "We'll begin with the bird chorus that will sing before the ceremony. All you other performers..." her eyes cut directly to Degrit and Katy, "will need to be silent so that we can have a successful rehearsal."

Degrit put his finger over his lips and glared at Katy as if to shush her. She smirked and nodded. They sat in white folding chairs listening to a chorus of snow white birds singing several beautiful songs that Katy had never heard.

When they finished, the "audience" politely clapped, and Ms. Pinkington gestured toward Katy. She took a deep breath and rose from her seat. Degrit walked her to the stage, which she thought seemed a bit strange, but thoughtful.

She had rehearsed with the lute player several times. She was to recite the poem as he plucked the melody softly in the background. She signaled to the lute player while Degrit lingered next to her.

The melody began softly behind her, and she took a deep breath to steady herself.

"Alas, my love, I hold only to you," she began. Before she could start the next line, she heard a clear, strong voice behind her sing the very words she had just spoken, in a melody that had become quite familiar to her. She turned and saw the last word escape from Degrit's lips. Katy's mouth fell open, and her eyes stared at him in disbelief.

The lute player played her cue twice, but she didn't notice. Ms. Pinkington clapped her wings yet again.

"Hold it, hold it," she shouted. "Katy, dear, shall we run over the plan again?" She gently latched onto Katy's arm and pointed toward the lute player. "Wallis will be playing the introduction. You will come in and recite the first line. Degrit will sing each line after you recite it."

71

She looked up into Katy's face. "Are you ready to have another go?" she asked. Katy nodded.

Ms. Pinkington stepped off the stage, and the lute player started up again. This time Katy didn't take her eyes off of Degrit. She recited the first line again, and Degrit winked at her as he opened his mouth to sing.

His perfect voice resonated in the courtyard, and Katy felt the words she was saying for the first time.

"You alone know my heart," she recited and was quickly echoed by Degrit. Their voices blended over each other at times and created something unexpected. When the last note was played, the crowd in the courtyard was silent for several long moments before standing to their feet and offering thunderous applause. When Katy looked out, she saw that the crowd had grown substantially. Apparently anyone in earshot of the palace had come in to listen.

The trio bowed graciously and then moved off the stage to make way for the next set of performances. Katy grabbed Degrit's hand and pulled him just outside of the courtyard with her.

"Why didn't you tell me you could sing like that?" she asked.

"You never asked."

Her arms were folded in mock anger. "And how long have you been planning to sing with me?" she asked.

"Eisley asked me months ago. She had the idea when she heard you practicing with Wallis one day. She came to me and suggested that I echo you with singing, and you know, I had a little bit of a crush on you, so I agreed." He pulled her to him. She wrapped her arms around his neck.

"You have the most amazing voice I've ever heard. Will you sing to me all the time?" she asked. She could feel his heart beating with hers as she snuggled up to him against the cold.

"All the time? I think that might get old fast, but I'll sing for you whenever you want me to. I'm glad you like it." Just at that moment Waith slithered up beside them. They released the hug and stood close together as they acknowledged Waith.

"Miss Katy and Mr. Degrit, I was just hearing your performance from the window and I must say it was absolutely beautiful. Your voices are blending perfectly."

"Thank you, Waith," Katy said, "that's very kind."

"Yes, thank you very much, Waith," Degrit added. Waith bowed his head slightly and slithered toward the courtyard.

"Come on, we better get back in the courtyard or Ms. Pinkington might have our heads." Degrit warned. Katy stood firm and grabbed his hand.

"Degrit...thank you," she said.

"For what?" he asked. She looked down at her hands that were enveloping Degrit's.

"I was so nervous and I felt awful that I couldn't sing. I knew that was the traditional wedding song, and I was sure Eisley would want it sung, but I just couldn't do it and I felt so badly that I..." Degrit interrupted her with a light kiss on the lips.

"You're welcome," he said, then led her back into the courtyard.

CHAPTER 16

KATY sat down at the table that was beautifully set with china of all different colors and types. The room was showered with snowflakes and the branches of a tree that vaguely resembled an evergreen. She was having tea with her mother and Eisley.

The Queen had decided that this was one of their last chances to be together as a family before the wedding, and she wanted to do something special.

Lutwidge came into the room, followed by three other valets. They all carried large trays full of beautiful cakes, fruits, cheeses, and other delectables. They unloaded the trays onto the table, then bowed and left the room.

The Queen picked up one of the teapots and began pouring tea for Eisley and Katy.

"My beautiful girls, this is perhaps the last chance we shall have to be together, just the three of us as we are now. Time is passing. New seasons are beginning. I wanted to stop the busyness for a moment so that I could look at you both and just be with you," she said. Eisley's eyes were misty, and she laid her hand on her mother's.

"Mother, thank you...for everything. This is beautiful, and I am so glad to have these moments with you and Katylove," Eisley said.

Katy realized that things really were about to change. She felt a pang of sadness to lose anything that she held so dear now. This family was her world. She tried to think of it as gaining a brother, but she knew things would be different, and that felt frightening. Eisley would be living away from the castle for the first year. She had a beautiful cabin a half day's ride away that was in a secluded part of the forest, surrounded by song trees and flowers. Thaddeus had been making sure the place was perfect. He'd had all the toxic and dangerous plants ripped out and replaced with things of beauty.

Katy and Eisley had gone to the cabin a couple of weeks ago so that Katy could see it. It was a beautiful place and seemed like it suited Eisley to a tee. Katy knew that she would miss her desperately. It was not a far ride to see her, but it was not at all the same as having her right there in the castle. She wiped a tear from her eye and began to pass the pastel cakes to her mother.

This tea was a memory that she wanted to keep in a jar in her heart (as Degrit had put it). She wanted to have this moment and hold it with both hands. When it was over Eisley hugged her tightly and kissed her cheek before she was whisked off by Ms. Pinkington.

The Queen lingered and invited Katy to sit in a seat just next to her. Katy gladly changed seats. The Queen's expression changed, and she looked around her to make sure they were alone.

"Katy, I have to talk to you in a very serious manner," she said. Katy nodded. Her stomach tightened a little. She had never seen the Queen act like this, and it made her more than a little distressed to see it.

"I am...concerned...about Eisley's match. I know that she loves him with all her heart and she's happy, which I love to see. But..." she let out a long sigh and shook her head, "something inside me will not let me be at peace. He's a charming young man, and I have seen or heard nothing to tell me otherwise, but I can barely sleep these days. My heart is not at rest." She put both her hands on Katy's. "Darling, tell me, what do you feel? Have you seen anything? Is it just old age or a mother who cannot let go?"

"Mother, I'm so sorry to hear of your distress. I think Thaddeus is a fine match for Eisley. He seems like a good man." She didn't feel like him not liking her could be called a character flaw; after all, in the Shadowlands, that was a common sentiment. "But Mother, if you are worried, perhaps you should talk with her about it." The Queen's brow furrowed. She nodded and leaned back against her chair.

"I must give her a way out if she wants it. I must tell her of my concerns, and then if she chooses to marry him anyway we must be full of nothing but joy for her." She patted Katy's hand, then forced a smile. "Don't worry another moment, Katylove. I'll have words with Eisley. Everything will be as it should be," she said.

* * *

Katy did worry. She couldn't stop. She ran to find Degrit later that afternoon. He was in the stable with his father. He came out to meet her.

"What's going on?" he asked.

"Can I talk to you alone?" She panted from running. He nodded, then gestured to his Dad that he was leaving for a moment. He put his arm around Katy and led her toward a secluded area in the forest.

"I'm sorry. I didn't know you were with your father. I didn't mean to interrupt," she said.

"Oh," he waved his hand nonchalantly, "don't worry about that. He just needed some extra help. With the wedding coming, he's had lots of extra work, and he asked me if I would come. At least it gives us something to talk about. Although I'm not very fond of horses." Katy looked at him in surprise. "Since my Mom's accident I haven't really had warm fuzzies toward them. But I'm excellent at mucking out stalls and throwing hay around." She pulled a long piece of hay out of his wild blond hair.

He sat her down on the bench in the woods.

"Are you all right? What did you need to talk about?" he asked. Katy recounted the entire conversation and what she had remembered...that look from Thaddeus. Degrit's face remained very solemn.

"I'm so worried! I don't know what's going to happen! What if he really is the wrong man for her, or what if she gets angry at Mother for suggesting such a thing?" She tipped her head over and laid it on his shoulder.

"I don't know Eisley as well as you, but she has never struck me as someone who gets angry easily. And I have never heard the Queen speak words that didn't seem absolutely fitting. I'm sure she will know just what to say without injuring Eisley." He rubbed her arm. "Besides, if the wedding is canceled, we can have one heck of a Christmas party instead." Katy nodded and smiled. She was so glad to have Degrit, and she felt his peace resting on her, but a tiny knot still remained in her stomach and absolutely refused to budge. She couldn't help but feel like this was all somehow her fault. Perhaps Thaddeus' dislike of her was tainting his personality. She must try very hard to do better, to be better, to be more likable. She would fight for peace in her family even

77

if it meant she had to disappear a little.

CHAPTER 17

THE morning of the wedding arrived with snow resting on the ground and sun shining in the sky. Katy was thankful for the perfect weather. She hoped the day would be nothing less than perfect as well.

The Queen had visited her room a few nights ago to reassure her that she had spoken with Eisley and everything was all right. The Queen advised Katy to forget all they had spoken of and be exceedingly happy for Eisley.

Katy had relaxed a bit. She'd slept well. This morning, however, she was struck with an awful case of nerves. She felt like she had an entire field of bread-and-butterflies fluttering around in her stomach. She began the process of getting dressed. She smiled at the sparkling pink dress that Eisley had picked for her. Light and delicate, it hugged her curves. She was just lacing up her boots when she heard a knock at the door.

"Come in," she said. Lutwidge peeked around the door. He entered, carrying a small tray with a hot cup of tea and an envelope.

"G-g-g-good m-m-morning, M-m-miss K-katy. I have a m-m-message f-f-for you. And something to w-warm you up." He smiled and moved the tray toward her.

"Oh, thank you so much, Lutwidge. You are so very thoughtful." He blushed through his scaly skin and bowed as he left the room.

Katy set the tea on her dresser and opened the envelope. There was a note written on a beautiful piece of parchment that had pressed reedia flowers in it. She held it to her nose and inhaled. She could still smell the hint of clove and sandalwood. She read the words inside:

To my dear Raven,

I know you must be nervous this morning, but I will be with you every moment. I wanted to send you this note because I couldn't wait until this afternoon to remind you that I love you with all that I am. I can hardly sleep nights. My mind is preoccupied with thinking about you. I feel that I am more myself with you than I have ever been even with myself. You are like a writing desk that I can pour my heart out on, writing every word that I've kept hidden inside. You are the Queen of my heart and I will never stop loving you.

Your,
Degrit

Katy sat on the red velvety couch and sipped her tea. Then she read the note over and over again. She felt warmth cover her. She wasn't sure if it was the tea or the note, but she was grateful for the peace it brought her.

* * *

Once Katy left her room, the morning flew by in a sort of crazed hurricane. Creatures were running here and there, helping with dressing and fetching things for Eisley.

Eisley was blissful. She wasn't panicked or anxious. She was a picture of the peaceful, happy bride. She sat in the chair, sighing and smiling off into the distance.

Ms. Pinkington was another story. She was an absolute mess, shouting orders at anyone who came within earshot and talking to herself nonstop. Katy wondered how many feathers she had lost. After finding so many on the floor, Katy had found a vase and begun collecting them to amuse herself and keep from being assigned any more jobs.

When the time came, Katy kissed Eisley on the cheek and rushed out to her seat near the front to be ready for Eisley's entrance. Degrit was already there. He was dressed in a deep blue velvet suit with a top hat. He looked distinguished and grown up.

"You look beautiful," he whispered. She blushed.

"Thank you. And thank you for the note. I think I have it memorized now," she said. He smiled. The chorus of birds was nearly done, and Katy took a deep breath to calm herself.

She walked to the front with Degrit and Wallis as the birds fluttered away. She began with the first line and then caught sight of Eisley walking down the center aisle. She almost forgot the next words. Eisley was breathtaking. Her dress trailed behind her and cascaded down in sparkling threads of silver, blue, and white. Katy felt her eyes misting and attempted to recite her lines without emotion compromising her voice.

When the song was over, Degrit led her to her seat. She made use of Degrit's handkerchief that he had kindly handed over as soon as they were seated. Her eyes wouldn't seem to dry up. She was so full of love for her family and aware of how different things could be.

When the ceremony was over, there was a time of mingling and chatting among the guests as those involved in the wedding moved into a large hall where the party to end all parties was to happen. The guests were to stay outside and mingle until an announcement was made that they were allowed to enter.

Degrit stayed out with the guests since his part was over. Katy wandered through the castle toward the hall, swinging her bouquet and feeling very sentimental. She walked the back way to avoid small talk and give her face a rest from smiling.

As she walked past the throne room, she found it odd that the door was shut. A strange and unpleasant feeling tugged at her. She thought she heard something. She put her hand against the door and paused there for a moment. Laughter echoed down the corridor from the party. Katy turned and began walking toward it, but the feeling wouldn't leave her alone.

She turned and walked back to the door again and pushed it open enough to poke her head in. And that was when she saw the sight that she tried for many years after to forget. Thaddeus was standing over something. His back was to her, she couldn't quite make out what was under him. He lifted his arm and Katy saw a blood-stained blade in his hand. She moved forward just enough to see what that pile of blue was underneath him.

A sudden wave of heavy nausea hit her. It was the Queen. Katy recognized the fabric of her dress, the shimmering blue that they had picked out together, the same blue threads that were woven into Eisley's dress. She was pinned down between Thaddeus's legs and blood was pooling on the ground next to her. Katy heard a piercing scream and realized as she put her hand to her chest that it was coming from her throat. Thaddeus turned. His face was splattered with blood and his eyes were full of hate.

"Grab her," he yelled. She looked to her left in just enough time to see a black bear barreling toward her. He grabbed her from behind and held her arms tight against her chest.

"I thought you said nobody would come this way, that we would have plenty of time to do the deed and get out before anyone even found her!" the bear growled at Thaddeus. "What are we supposed to do now?"

Thaddeus stood up and wiped the blood off his face with his black sleeve. He had insisted on wearing all black, saying it was classier. Katy understood his real motive now. Her mother's body shifted abruptly as Thaddeus stood and kicked her out of his way. Tears poured from Katy's eyes. She felt sobs escaping, though no sound came out. Her mouth was entirely encased in a large bear paw.

"Well, Miss Katylove," Thaddeus said as he strutted toward her. "Wasn't counting on getting two for the price of one today. I guess it's my lucky day. I'll be running this kingdom sooner than I thought." He held the blade that still dripped her mother's blood to her neck.

"N-not likely," Lutwidge's voice boomed with all the confidence he could muster. Something hit Thaddeus in the head at that moment. Lutwidge must have thrown something at him. He fell backward. The blade he held sliced into Katy's jaw as he lost his balance. The bear pushed her away and attempted to run, but when he turned he was faced with more than just Lutwidge. The doorway was crowded with creatures that had been near the throne room when Katy had let out that involuntary scream.

She scrambled to her feet and ran to her mother's body. The bear fought his way out of the crowd, but was later caught by the griffin and had but a few short moments before his story was ended.

Katy hugged her mother to her chest. Her throat had been slit and blood covered the front of her perfect blue dress and framed her body. Her face was peaceful and pale. Katy heard herself sobbing and saying "no" over and over, but it was like listening to someone else. This couldn't be real. She kept telling herself that this was a bad dream.

The crowd had surrounded Thaddeus and tied him to a chair. Some of the larger animals carried him (chair and all) down to the long-empty dungeons. The cell was locked, and he was left with only an angry badger for company. The badger marched back and forth as he imagined a guard was supposed to do. The keys were in the care of Lutwidge. He had proved himself to have more courage than even he had imagined.

Katy heard Degrit's voice through a fog. She was lost. She still held her mother's body. She was covered in blood, her own mingling with that of her mother's, sinking fast into shock and despair. She looked up to see him running toward her. His face was desperate.

"Katy...Katy," he ran to her side and took her face in his hands. He saw the wound on her jaw and shouted for the healer. He tore the hem from his shirt and held it firmly against the cut.

"Degrit...my mother...help me..." she stammered. His eyes filled and he blinked back tears as he took her in his arms.

"Oh, my Katylove, how I wish I could," he said. He could see that Katy was in shock and would not leave her mother's side anytime soon without some help. "Katy, the Queen is past our help. She is running to meet her love now. Come. She would want you to get that cut taken care of." Katy allowed him to pull her off her mother and walk her out. Her eyes stayed on the Queen until they were out of the room.

"Eisley! Oh, God!!" Katy's sister came back into her mind like a jolt and she found her feet and ran. Degrit was right on her heels. He caught her arm just as she neared the Hall where Eisley was visiting with guests, oblivious to the fact that her life had just shattered into a million pieces.

"Katy, let me go to her," Degrit pleaded. "If she saw you right now...the shock would be too much." Katy looked down at her once pink dress now splattered in dark red. She turned her hands over and saw that they also were wet with her blood...or was it her mother's? "I'll break it to her gently," he said.

Lutwidge was coming up the passage behind them with the healer in tow. "Go with Lutwidge and the healer. I'll take care of Eisley. I'll be right back to you. When you are cleaned up we will bring Eisley to you." Katy nodded and started to turn toward Lutwidge. Degrit grabbed her before she turned and kissed her. "I'm so sorry." She felt new tears rolling down her cheeks. Lutwidge put his thin arm around her shoulders and led her to a parlor where the healer could tend to her wound. She felt cold. She wondered if she could ever feel warm again.

CHAPTER 18

KATY sat in an embroidered high back chair that she had seen her mother in many times. She traced the yellow stitches on the arm with her finger over and over. The healer had to clean her entire face and neck before beginning. The blood seemed to be everywhere. Once Katy was cleaned up, the healer began pounding an herbal concoction in her mortar.

The healer was an old frog with a strangely human-like face. A threadbare purple cloak that wrapped around her head and hung down past her knees was her usual attire. She rarely spoke. Her eyes were full of compassion as she applied a greenish-black goo to Katy's jaw. Ms. Pinkington patted her hand. She had been brought in to assist as Lutwidge had to attend to sending the guests back to their homes. It seemed as though all of Ms. Pinkington's energy had been used up in the ceremony. She was almost calm now.

"That's to numb you so you won't feel the pain, dear," she said.

Why bother? thought Katy. *I couldn't feel anything right now if I wanted to.* The healer sat down in a seat near Katy and began preparing the items she needed next.

"She has to wait a few minutes for the poultice to work before she sews you up. Shall we get you out of that dress while we wait?" Katy glanced down at her bloodsoaked dress and then nodded vigorously.

Ms. Pinkington helped her pull the dress down around her waist and then she stepped out of it. The blood had even saturated her underclothes and Katy practically tore them off. Ms. Pinkington walked over with a pure white nightdress and Katy was grateful for it, not even the slightest stain upon it. She washed herself off with a damp towel, then stepped in and pulled it up over her shoulders. It made her feel clean. Ms. Pinkington tied the back and then sat her in the chair again.

The blood-stained clothes were gone. Ms. Pinkington was nothing if not efficient. Katy had a fleeting thought that she wanted to cling to those clothes. Her mother's blood was on that fabric and she wanted to hold on to it, but the sane part of her brain knew that was ridiculous. Ms. Pinkington threw a soft brown blanket across Katy's lap and was there patting her hand again.

The healer came over and began cleaning out the poultice and preparing the wound for being stitched. There was a knock. Ms. Pinkington went to the door. There was whispering for a moment. "Yes, she's all cleaned up now, but she hasn't been stitched up yet," Ms. Pinkington whispered.

She glanced over at Katy and then opened the door wide. Degrit and Eisley stood in the doorway. Eisley was white as a sheet and her eyes were still dry. The horror of this reality had refused to allow her to believe it. Now she saw Katy sitting expressionless and white in her mother's chair. The healer was sewing up a gaping wound on her face. The reality hit her hard and she ran to Katy. She knelt beside her and sobbed. Katy rubbed her hair. She felt a single tear roll down her cheek. She wished for more, but none came now.

"Oh, Katylove, it can't be true. No, it just can't be. Tell me it's not true," Eisley begged.

"Eisley...she's gone...she's gone," Katy whispered.

Eisley sobbed harder. "Katy, are you sure it was Thaddeus? Maybe you were mistaken?" Katy felt hate rise in her throat at the mention of his name, but looking into her sister's eyes she felt compassion for her.

"Eisley, I'm sorry for you, more than you will know, but it was undoubtedly Thaddeus." She spat out his name with venom. "His blade was at my neck ready to send me into Mother's arms. He is not who you knew him to be."

Degrit watched her from the doorway. Concern had overtaken his laughing eyes. She looked intently at him as she stroked a sobbing Eisley's hair. She had lost her mother, but Eisley — she had lost her mother and her love on what was supposed to be the happiest day of her life. She had been horribly betrayed by the one she trusted the most. Katy couldn't stop thinking that she was so glad she was the one who walked in on that scene. Eisley would never have recovered. Katy wondered if she would.

That pause was haunting her. Why had she stopped outside the door? Why didn't she open it right away? If she had acted sooner her mother might still be alive. She captured her thoughts and shoved them to the back of her mind to deal with later. She had to take care of Eisley now.

* * *

The healer had finished the stitches, then given Eisley a strong herbal tea that would let her have a long healing sleep. Katy refused it.

The old frog left some beside her chair just in case she changed her mind.

Eisley was sleeping peacefully in her room and Katy stood in her doorway watching. She felt Degrit's arm on her lower back.

"She's alright for now," he whispered. "Come on, you need some rest too." She let him lead her to her bedroom.

She started backing out as the colors in the room filled her eyes. "I can't do it," she said. "It's too red...it's just too...I just can't sleep in there." Degrit held her tight.

"It's alright, love, this is a palace. There are many rooms. We'll find the right one." They started down hallways looking into different rooms. All the guest rooms had been cleared out for the safety and privacy of the royal family. Those who had come from far away for the wedding were matched with local families and all were found places to stay until they could journey home.

They found a room not far from Eisley's that was decorated in browns and tans. Katy climbed into the bed. Degrit sat next to her.

"Do you want me to stay?" he asked. She grabbed his hand.

"Would you, please?" She looked desperate.

"Of course," he answered. She rolled over on her side. Degrit stayed on top of the blankets fully clothed. He moved as close to her as he could and embraced her. They lay in silence for a long time, and then Katy felt the dam breaking. The sobs that had earlier abandoned her in favor of shock now found her again.

She sobbed for what felt like an eternity. Degrit held her tight and kissed her hair. He whispered words of love to her like little prayers. She found sleep just before the sun came up. Then Degrit wept for Katy.

CHAPTER 19

KATY felt like time had been altered in some fashion. The days seem to crawl by. She kept hoping that she would wake one morning and it would be six months down the road.

Waith had been a godsend. He came and wept with her for the first week or so. He helped plan and facilitate the funeral. Then they got down to the business of doing what must be done to keep the kingdom running smoothly. Things had to be decided. Change was forced upon them.

One of the first changes was the addition of security. Guards were recruited from all over the kingdom. When Katy had first arrived, the palace was open and inviting. There was no fear of attack or betrayal. Thaddeus and his plotters had tainted Wonderland with their lust for blood and power.

Lutwidge had volunteered to be in charge of security. He developed a rigorous exam for the candidates who wished to be the Queen's guard. He was also an impeccable judge of character. Everyone at the palace felt confident with him in charge.

Katy spent any free time she had with Degrit. He was the salve for her soul. He made her feel that somehow things would work out. She knew that she might not ever be able to find the she that she used to be, but she hoped that this new she that was emerging would be stronger and somehow better.

Degrit worried about her. She had grown a little colder and there was a tenderness that had been lost. He didn't feel that he had access to her whole heart anymore. He held on to faith that he could help her find her way back to him.

Eisley tried to fully engage in all the decisions being made, but found it difficult to concentrate. She had gone to the dungeon once with Lutwidge to visit Thaddeus and see for herself. He had refused to speak to her. Her heart cracked on that day, and she never quite recovered.

Waith and Katy had spent hours discussing the future of the kingdom. Waith thought that Eisley was no longer fit to rule, but Katy insisted that they rule together. The kingdom at large had already started to refer to Eisley as the White Queen. They couldn't seem to get that wedding day image out of their minds. The White Queen was a suitable name for Eisley. She was pure and innocent. Even after losing some of her sanity, she never lost her kindness.

Katy was dubbed the Queen of Hearts by a persistent Degrit who went so far as to show the playing card to Waith and point out the resemblance. She felt a pang of dishonesty being called something that alluded to compassion and love when she thought of the thorn of hate that had lodged itself in her heart.

* * *

Katy watched the guards training and being fitted for uniforms in the courtyard. Waith had uniforms designed to look like the other playing cards in the deck. Katy had not objected because she didn't really care what the guards looked like, so long as they protected the ones she loved. Now, looking down at the pack of playing cards wielding long spears, she found it more than a little comical.

She was back in her own room again. Sitting on the velvety couch gave her a good view out the window into the courtyard and surrounding forest. She held Degrit's note in her hand, the note that calmed her the morning of the wedding. It had lost its scent and was worn to a thin ghost of a letter. She read it over and over. It always brought a bittersweet feeling. The words filled her leaking heart with something to hope in, but she couldn't help remembering the morning she first read them and the warmth she had felt. Now a coolness had settled around her and didn't seem to want to leave.

She saw Degrit come into the courtyard. He gave Lutwidge a hearty pat on the back. She tucked the note into a little box on her dresser and headed down to meet him.

"Katy, I am taking you away," he said when he saw her coming down the stairs toward him.

"What?"

"I am taking you away for the day. You have been immersed in all of this without one moment away. I think it is time you have a little respite." He held out his hand to lead her. She started to protest and tell him how many things she had to do and how she couldn't leave now, but she saw Waith standing behind Degrit pointing with his tail toward the door. She smiled at him and took Degrit's hand.

He led her to the stable.

"I thought you were afraid of horses," she said.

He nodded. "I am, but I thought if I was going to try to help you, I should be willing to let you help me." He looked nervous and excited.

"Besides, it would take too long to walk where I want to take you. So can I ride with you on Fleetfoot?" he asked.

"Of course," she answered. Degrit's father, Tomas, was standing outside the stable with Fleetfoot's reigns held loosely in his hand. He was strong and kind. He smiled, but it never reached his eyes. Katy took the reigns and thanked him. Degrit nodded to him.

Katy mounted and held her hand down to Degrit to help him up. He took a deep breath.

"Believe it or not, I used to be quite good with horses. I spent much of my childhood riding through the forest bareback," he said.

"Why does that not surprise me?" Katy said. "Are you going to stand there and talk or are you going to get on the horse?" He raised an eyebrow at her and took her hand. He landed in the saddle behind her and she felt him let out another deep breath.

She wrapped his arms around her waist and gave Fleetfoot a gentle nudge. Degrit pulled himself tight into Katy's back. She put her free hand over his arms that were encircling her waist and rubbed them.

He was quiet as they rode out into the forest. She could hear only his breathing. She stopped when they neared the Vast Meadowlands.

She turned herself in the saddle and looked at him. He sat up and returned her gaze. She could see that he had been crying. She rubbed his cheek and wiped away the tears.

"I'm sorry..." he said. He held her gaze.

"Don't be," she answered, assuming he apologized for his tears.

"No...I'm sorry...for you. I know the pain of losing your mother. Being on this animal has brought it all back." He breathed in deeply. "But I wasn't there when my mother fell. I didn't have to see her last moments. I can't imagine how difficult this must be for you. I'm so sorry. I wish I could have protected you somehow." Tears continued to fall from his eyes.

Katy was undone by his tenderness. She fought back her own tears and kissed him. When she started to pull away he grabbed her and kissed her again. His hands held her face close to his.

"Well, that should certainly change my opinion of horses," he whispered. She laughed with him and was glad to move past the tears.

"You, sir, have not told me where we are going."

"Ah, yes..." he wiped his eyes and attempted to regain his composure. "I have a gift for you, but we have to go pick it up. It is far north of here. Ride straight north until you feel very confused as to where you are and then you're nearly there." She furrowed her brow and looked at him with uncertainty. He smiled and raised an eyebrow.

"Hold on," she said in just enough time for him to grab her before they were galloping north at full speed. He laughed and held tight to her.

CHAPTER 20

THE sun had changed positions in the sky, and Katy suddenly began to feel very disoriented. She pulled back on Fleetfoot's reigns and looked around.

"You're nearly there," Degrit whispered. She laughed, remembering his instructions. A little nudge and Fleetfoot was off again.

They came to a sign and Degrit signaled that this was the place. Katy couldn't read this sign. She recognized the letters, but they seemed to be in an order that made no sense. When she looked again it seemed that they had rearranged themselves and now read "Don't Eat Purple Glots". She tied Fleetfoot to the fence and grabbed Degrit's arm to walk with him.

"I must warn you," he started, "North Wonderland is different. I know you haven't been here before, but creatures from this area tend to be a bit...well...mad." Katy leaned back in surprise and looked at him. He smirked.

A plump pigeon greeted them at the gate. He bowed dramatically.

"Welcome, Your Majesty," he said.

"Thank you," Katy said.

"I wasn't talking to you!" The pigeon glanced at her in irritation and let out a fast breath of annoyance. Degrit bit his lip and his eyes widened. Katy put her fingers over her mouth until the laughter threatening to escape had subsided.

"I beg your pardon," she said to the sincerely ticked off bird.

"Yeah, you do, don't you? Well, come in, I've made some purple glots. They're best eaten while they are still hot." Katy looked at Degrit with concern. He seemed unphased as he pulled her along.

The pigeon's home was a bit like a nest on the ground. It was all twigs and twine wrapped around and around until it made a nice little cave. They stepped through the door and found that it was surprisingly cozy inside. It seemed like a normal little house, although there were some major differences. For instance, the furniture and appliances were attached to the walls instead of sitting on the floor. This caused the pigeon to have to flutter as he opened the oven to retrieve the purple glots. Katy wasn't certain that she or Degrit would be able to access the sofa at all. They stood in the center of the room on a large fuzzy rug.

"Sit, go on, sit," the pigeon said, as he fluttered about in the small space. Degrit eyed the couch and the twig wall next to it.

"I think we can manage," he whispered. He used the twigs and twine as a sort of ladder, then turned to help Katy up the same way. Once they were seated with their legs dangling in the air, the pigeon fluttered over with a tray of yellow cakes and tea. He pulled around a table that was attached to the sofa. It reminded Katy of a school desk. He sat the tray in front of them and passed each of them a little plate. They nodded politely.

"Purple glot?" he asked Degrit. Degrit nodded and smiled. The pigeon used his feathers like a little spatula. He scooped up a small yellow cake and put it on Degrit's plate. He then poured him a cup of milk with a tiny splash of tea in it. He completely ignored Katy till Degrit cleared his throat. "Oh, I suppose you can have some too," he muttered toward Katy. Degrit served her, as it seemed the pigeon was not going to have anything to do with her.

The cake was yellow and spongy. It tasted like spun sugar and cream. Katy didn't understand why it was called purple glot and wasn't even sure what glot was.

"So, tell me, Your Majesty. How are things in the kingdom? How is the Queen?" the pigeon asked.

"Flucial, I've told you many times before. My mother is not the Queen. She merely worked in the castle. And I'm sure you are aware that my mother died some years ago."

The pigeon shook his head several times. "Of course I knew that, you silly boy. How is the glot?" Flucial seemed to be disoriented and attempting to get himself back on track.

"It's delicious," offered Katy.

"I didn't ask you!" Flucial shouted. Degrit put a hand on her leg.

"Flucial, I'm here to see Jesib. Do you know where she might be?"

The pigeon fluttered around for no apparent reason causing an awful disturbance for such a small space. "I know that you are here to see Jesib! Do you think I am mad?" he shouted. Katy bit her bottom lip. "Follow me," he said.

Degrit slid the table out of the way, then climbed down and helped Katy do the same. The pigeon flew out the front door and vanished into the woods. He was gone before they had a chance to follow him.

"I don't think he liked me much," Katy said when it was clear that they were on their own. Degrit laughed.

"No, I don't suppose he did. I did try to warn you. Welcome to North Wonderland. Don't worry, I think I know how to find Jesib."

Katy wasn't worried so much about finding Jesib. She was more worried about what she would encounter when she met Jesib.

* * *

After they had walked a bit deeper into the forest, Degrit took out several yellow cakes he had hidden in his pocket. He set them on the ground, then sat with his back against an old gnarled tree. Katy went over and joined him. She was nearly dozing off when Degrit jumped up suddenly.

A large purple and grey cat was standing over the cakes, picking them up one by one and putting them into her handbag.

"Jesib!" Degrit said. She vanished completely. Katy sucked in her breath. "Jesib, it's me, Degrit. You were great friends with my father, Tomas. I need to speak with you. Please, show yourself." Katy looked where the cat had been and the purple stripes began to come into focus, followed by the grey ones, and then the whole of the cat. Katy had never seen anything quite like it.

"Degrit, is it really you?" Jesib looked at him in wonder. He nodded. "It's been so long. I heard that your mother met her end. I am truly sorry. How is your father?" she asked.

Degrit sighed. "He still works at the palace. He lives in body, but his soul left with mother's."

Jesib nodded and then shook her head sympathetically. Then, as if suddenly remembering her affection for him, she took Degrit in her arms and hugged him passionately.

"It is good to see you," she said as she held him out to look at him. "What brings you to The North?" He cut his eyes toward Katy and then leaned in closer to the cat to whisper. She nodded and made little sounds of agreement as he shared his secret plans with Jesib. "Yes,

98

that's a most agreeable idea." She turned and smiled at Katy. "You must be the daughter of the Queen. Katy, is it?" Katy felt the pain of loss again at the mention of her mother, but buried it deep in her stomach. She stood and nodded, then shook Jesib's hand.

"It's very nice to meet you, Jesib." She was quite relieved by how sane this cat appeared to be.

"And you," Jesib replied. "Well, we should start on our way. Follow me." She got down on all fours and headed into the forest. Katy and Degrit started after her. She turned and looked at them in shock. "Not that way!" she said. "Like this." She pushed down on Degrit's back to show that she intended for them to walk on all fours like her.

Degrit looked over at Katy and shrugged. She took back all the sanity she had assumed Jesib possessed. She felt thankful that she had worn such a long dress.

It wasn't far to Jesib's house, but Degrit and Katy were both quite winded from going on all fours through the forest. They collapsed onto Jesib's front steps while she went in to get them drinks. Degrit and Katy tried to quiet their giggles so they wouldn't offend their hostess.

Jesib emerged from the house with saucers of milk. Katy was unsure as to how she should proceed. She watched as Degrit graciously began to lap up the milk like an animal. She gave him a questioning look and he answered with his eyes that she should do the same. She took a couple licks and then placed it beside her on the step.

"I'll be back in just a moment," Jesib said. "I know you must hurry off on your journey. You don't want to be stuck in the North at night. You would lose your way for certain and may have to wait till daylight to get home." She started back into the house.

"Thank you," Degrit called after her. Katy eyed him suspiciously. "Don't worry. We'll be on our way momentarily," he assured her.

In just a few moments Jesib came back out with a grey sack that was wriggling as though it were alive or contained something alive. Degrit hugged and thanked her, and Katy curtsied and again stated that it had been nice to have met her. Jesib stood on the porch, waving to them, and so they headed off on all fours. They carried on this way (with Degrit trying to carry the grey bag and walk about on threes) until they were certain they were out of sight. Then they stood up and walked as humans again, which came as a great relief to both of them.

CHAPTER 21

ONCE Katy and Degrit untied Fleetfoot and started in a southward direction, it wasn't long before they were out of the area known as North Wonderland. Katy felt the cloud of confusion lift.

"No wonder the people there are mad," she said. "I feel a weight has lifted just being away from there."

"It's strange, isn't it?" Degrit responded. "I once took Flucial with me on an outing to the Vast Meadowland, and he claimed it felt no different to him there than it did in the North. It must change you somehow after so much time."

"Very strange," Katy said. She thought back to the unusual encounters they had just experienced and started to giggle. Degrit joined her and soon they were laughing so hard they were barely able to stay on Fleetfoot. It felt like rain falling on parched dry ground to Katy. They rode on until they had reached the edge of the Vast Meadowland.

"Stop here," Degrit said. Katy pulled back on the reigns and they both jumped down and sat in the soft grass. Fleetfoot wandered the meadow, snacking on the long green strands.

Degrit held the sack up to Katy while trying to compose himself again. "This is a gift for you. I hope it gives you something to smile about now and then." Katy carefully set the bag on the grass, then untied the twine that held it shut. A tiny kitten crawled out of the sack. He was grey and purple like Jesib, but also had stripes of teal. He was so fluffy he was almost a ball instead of a kitten shape.

Katy melted. She picked him up and held him to her face. Much oohing and aahing and baby talk happened in the next few moments.

"Is he Jesib's?" she asked. She stroked his fur and kissed his face.

"No, he was left on her doorstep. She sent me a message to ask if I knew of a home for him. Her mind isn't always the best at remembering though. He is the same type of cat as Jesib, which means he will have vanishing powers. But they don't start vanishing until they are one or two years old — at least that's what Jesib told me," he said.

Katy set the little bundle down and hugged Degrit. "Thank you," she said. "You always seem to know what I need." They sat playing with the kitten until the sun started to get low in the sky.

"Would you mind if I took the reigns?" Degrit asked, looking over at Fleetfoot. Katy was thrilled that he was taking to riding again. He helped her get on behind him. She held the kitten on her chest and gently sandwiched him there against Degrit's back.

"Does he have a name?" she asked.

"No, that's your responsibility."

"I remember a place from the Shadowlands that I used to love visiting. I think it was called Cheshire. Some of my best memories of that dark land were there. So it seems a perfect name — happy memories in a dark place. He'll be Ches for short." She snuggled him to her face again.

Katy was so glad to have had a day full of thinking of other things.

She felt sunlight again. She remembered the color of the grass. She laughed at the absurdity of the North. She leaned against Degrit. He was breathing life into her again. She felt her heart beating for the first time since the Queen's death.

* * *

Cheshire was welcomed into the castle with open arms. Eisley and Waith were also delighted to have something to enjoy and laugh about. Ches was quite mischievous, and even without vanishing skills, he found ways to get into trouble almost constantly. Waith often feigned annoyance, but Katy always saw the smirk at the corners of his toothless mouth.

Eisley came down one morning with her wedding dress in one hand and Ches in the other. The dress had been shredded.

"Look! Just look at the kind service this sweet little dear has done for me. Now I have no reason to keep this dress, and I shall be forced to throw it away." She smiled from ear to ear. Katy laughed and came closer to inspect the dress. "Thank you, Ches. I am forever in your debt," Eisley said, and she kissed his head. They all had a good laugh that day and sat around ripping the dress further before they threw it out. It was a good feeling to have moments of joy seeping back in.

CHAPTER 22

EISLEY and Katy were enjoying a leisurely breakfast and laughing at Ches, who insisted on stepping in his saucer of cream as he drank. He would then spend long and tedious amounts of time licking that paw to make sure he got every ounce.

Waith slithered in, sucking on his bottom lip as he did when he had news he was nervous about delivering.

"What is it, Waith?" Eisley asked.

He sighed deeply. "I have an idea and I'm just not for certain about how you and Miss Katy will be reacting. But," he pressed on, "I have been thinking, and I believe that this kingdom is in desperate need of something worth celebrating." He cleared his throat. "Miss Katy is not quite seventeen. So no weddings on the horizon yet; besides, we may not be quite ready for a wedding. But alas, we have two beautiful Queens who are coming into power. We need a coronation. A celebration. A party to celebrate your new reign. We have all cried for Maureen's death." It was the first time Katy had ever heard Waith refer to her mother by her first name; his love for her was apparent. "But we need to see the dawning of an era that is new, a new beginning!"

Eisley smiled sweetly in Waith's direction. "That's a beautiful idea, Waith," she said.

Katy fidgeted and pulled at the corner of her napkin. "I...I don't know...I'm not sure I really want to be...I'm not sure that I'm ready for..." Katy trailed off. "Can I have a little time to think about it?" she asked. Waith nodded with a concerned look in his eyes.

Katy grabbed her coat and headed out the door. The weather had turned warmer and the snow was long gone, but the clouds looked ominous. She stopped when she came to the little bench in the forest. The ground felt cool as she sat in front of it, leaning her back against the cold marble. She took a deep breath and looked down at her hands shaking uncontrollably.

She wasn't ready to be a queen. There was no way she could do it. She wasn't even really of royal blood. She was not from this world. She was an alien who had stood and done nothing as her adopted mother was slaughtered. She felt tears begin to pour down her face, and sobs came from deep in her chest. If only she could be more like Eisley, more like Waith. She didn't believe she was capable of all they hoped for her. She knew that eventually she would let them down. She had begged Eisley to rule alone, but Eisley had refused, saying that they brought each other balance.

Katy gave herself over to raw emotion and fear. She curled up in the grass and sobbed. Her mind became blank. Time got hazy and she had no idea how long she had been there. She felt a hand touch her shoulder. Someone sat next to her and lifted her head onto his lap. She opened her eyes long enough to see Degrit's green eyes staring down at her. She buried her head in his lap and he stroked her hair. There were no words spoken for a very long time. Katy's sobbing eventually became just an occasional moan or sucking in of air, and the tears slowed to a trickle. She let out a long shaky sigh.

After some time she sat up next to Degrit. He pulled her against him and embraced her. She felt like a liar. Everyone believed her to be someone who deserved the throne, but she was an imposter.

The rain started slow at first, then harder and faster until she and Degrit were soaked through. He didn't rush her or try to move her. He took off his overcoat and wrapped it around her shoulders.

"I can't do this," she finally spoke. He brushed her cheek with his fingers and tucked a wet strand of hair behind her ear.

"Can't do what?" he asked. She shook her head and looked at her fingers. "Katy, let me in. I want to help you. It's killing me to see you in this pain." He held her without speaking for a long time. "I know it takes time. I have dark moments of grief for my mother, and it's been years now," he said.

Katy pushed against his chest so that she could look in his eyes. They were both soaked and rain was still falling hard.

"You don't understand..." she whispered. She stood up and turned her back to him, clutching her arms across her chest. Degrit took her and turned her toward him.

He stared at her until she looked up at him. "I love you. I'll stay until I do understand." She stood with rain dripping down her face and hair. She felt the walls she was trying so hard to build being torn down once again by this wild boy she had found in the woods. He could no longer be called a boy. She could see the muscles in his chest and arms as his white, rain-soaked shirt clung to him. He was much taller than she. His eyes were tamer now, with more wisdom behind them.

"I can't be a queen," she confessed. He looked into her eyes intently and let her continue. "I'm not even from here. I'm not the Queen's real daughter." She drew in a deep breath. When she spoke again, the words came fast and frantic. "I didn't stop him. I was right there. I just stood and screamed like an idiot. I just let him kill the mother who had first shown me love. I didn't deserve her. I never did. Eisley did. Eisley should be queen. I should be in the dungeon with him." She couldn't say Thaddeus' name. "I am not worthy of her crown."

Degrit tightened his grip on her arms.

"Your mother loved you, and she believed that you were hers. She believed in you. She expected you to rule someday." He shook her gently. "You are worthy. You are worthy of love, *my* love, Eisley's love, the love of the kingdom. You were born for this." He looked almost angry as he continued. "Your mother's death was NOT your fault. There was nothing you could have done! We were all powerless to stop it. We didn't see it coming. You nearly lost your own life that day." He ran his thumb across the scar along her jawline where Thaddeus' knife had sliced her. She shook her head and tried to free herself from him. "Katy, don't run away from me." He pulled her into his chest again. "I need you. Don't close me off. I wouldn't lie to you, Katy. You are exactly what this kingdom needs. Eisley can't rule alone." He squeezed her tighter. "I need you, Katy. You are exactly what *I* need. I can't bear to hear you speak so much hate about the girl that I am in love with."

Katy began to sob again. "I didn't think I had any tears left," she said between sobs. She let Degrit hold her and tried to let the truth he had spoken soak into her heart.

* * *

Degrit walked Katy back to the palace and made certain that she was dry and warm. Even after she was in dry clothes, drinking hot tea and sitting by a roaring fire, it took a long time before she stopped shivering. Degrit didn't leave her side that day. He slept on the red couch in her room that night. She felt safe again. She hoped she could hold on to the truth that Degrit had spoken over her. Truth seemed so slippery at times, and somehow the lies in her mind seemed as solid as rock. Degrit was the most solid thing in her life and she chose, for now, to hold to him.

CHAPTER 23

EISLEY and Waith eventually persuaded Katy to agree to the coronation party, with a little help from Degrit. It was announced in all the villages. There would be a celebration like none ever seen. It was to be held in the Vast Meadowlands and would last several days. The creatures of Wonderland were delighted to have something to look forward to. They had no trouble feeling loyalty toward their new Queens-to-be. They had adored their mother and felt certain that the new Queens would rule with the same compassion and wisdom. The excitement in the kingdom was palpable.

Katy dove head first into her responsibilities. She busied herself with anything she could find that needed to be done. Her mind was much kinder when it was distracted and couldn't be bothered to constantly accuse her.

Degrit had been snatched up by Waith to help with the planning and logistics of the upcoming celebration. It was to be held in the beginning of the warm months, nearly four months away. Degrit was bright and innovative and easily found solutions to situations that had Waith sucking his bottom lip and furrowing his brow. They were a great team. Waith worried and Degrit fixed.

Eisley was becoming the face of the palace. She found great joy in going out and visiting with her subjects. She was constantly taking soup to ill families, helping with community gardens, or reading to children. She found healing in giving to others.

Katy admired Eisley for all she did, but all the work that needed to be done at the palace seemed to be falling to Katy. She didn't really mind the busyness, but there were some jobs she would rather not do. The weekly hearings, for instance, were certainly not her favorite. Her mother had handled it with such grace and never complained. Katy almost believed that she had enjoyed it. She remembered going and watching that first time when she had seen Ms. Tweedle and the griffin. The Queen had always known the right thing to do. Katy felt, with every new issue that was brought before her, that she somehow lost wisdom and grew younger. She felt like a little girl playing dress up and sitting in her mother's giant throne. She wished there was someone else there to whisper the right answers to her.

Lutwidge came to the hearings one morning to ask for a date to be set to try Thaddeus and decide on his sentence. Katy decided that it must be after the coronation so that their authority would not be questioned, whatever decision they made. She set it for a month after. She knew it would be hard on Eisley (and herself), and she wanted to give them a little time to settle into their new roles before this was thrown at them. She felt a dagger of heat in her stomach anytime Thaddeus' name was mentioned, and she hoped that it would lessen by the time he was standing before her.

She hadn't seen him since the day she'd watched him kill her mother. It didn't seem right for her to risk seeing him for the first time at the trial. Her emotions might betray her and sap all her strength.

She needed to be strong and ready.

The next time Degrit was free, she asked if he would come with her to see Thaddeus. Since her mind would not be changed, he agreed.

* * *

The dungeon could have been much worse. It was clean and full of light. The beds were real beds, not just cots. They had not really ever been used. The paint was light yellow and looked brand new. The cells were all empty but one. Thaddeus' accomplice, the black bear, had been made into a very fine rug by the griffin and given to Lutwidge as a gift. He proudly placed it in the main room of his little cottage.

The guard at the door stood as he recognized Katy. He wore the uniform of a four of spades. Katy had eventually become accustomed to seeing playing cards throughout the castle. He bowed low. She could see beneath his helmet that he was an ape of some sort.

"Your Majesty? What can I do for you today?" he said, remaining bent over.

"I wish to speak with the prisoner," she said matter of factly. The ape looked up in surprise and concern, then glanced back at Degrit, who nodded.

"This way, ma'am. You can stand in the hallway and talk through the bars. That will be safer. But I must warn you. He is keen on spitting. Would you like me to stay in with you or wait outside?" he asked.

"We'll be fine. You can wait outside," Katy answered. She looked back at him and smiled. "Thank you."

He forced a smile and bowed out of the room. Degrit took a tight grasp of her hand and led her down the corridor to the last cell on the right. She let out a quiet sigh.

Thaddeus rose from the bed as he spotted them. He had been stripped of everything and wore only a simple white gown. "Oh, well, what an honor. Katy, the fake little sister princess come to visit," he began taunting. She felt Degrit pull back on her hand. He gave her an expression that asked if she was sure and she nodded.

"That scar is a beauty, my lady. I've made you even uglier than before. Didn't know that was possible," he snarled. His features were still the same. The red hair and freckles were still intact, but the boyish charm had vanished, and his face was contorted in a strong look of hate.

"Thaddeus, I have come to ask about your fellow conspirators. Was it just you and the bear, or were there others?" She stood perfectly erect and tried very hard to appear as if his words were empty to her.

"As if, as if I would tell you anything, Your Highness." He bowed in an exaggerated manner.

"Prontil, our seer, has been missing for months. I presume that you had something to do with this?" she asked, still holding hard to her composure.

"Oh, well, I'm not as dumb as I look, now am I? I couldn't have him giving away the game now could I?" He laughed and stuck his face through the bars to intimidate her. "See, there were parts that were easy and other parts that were not so easy. Squashing Prontil like the tiny insect that he was...that was easy. Eisley, that tasty little lamb, it wasn't hard to pretend to be in love with her, although I wouldn't call what I felt 'love.' And getting her to fall in love with me, well that was a cakewalk. You can see why, can't you?" He started with the insane laughter again. "You...you...Katylove," he said her name with revulsion, "you were not so easy. I never liked you. There was just something about that black hair. It's not natural. I hated to be near you. Oh, but sweet little Eisley just loves you so much and insisted on having you around. It was hardest to play the part when you were there. And I just couldn't wait to get my hands around the Queen's neck." Katy shuddered and gripped tighter to Degrit's hand.

"And you got to get a front row seat to the whole bloody event, didn't you, love?" he whispered in a raspy voice. "And you just stood there like a chess piece, like a helpless pawn waiting for someone to tell you to move. But you did manage a scream. Lot of good that did her. You were the bloody hero of the day, weren't you, love?" He ran his tongue over his cracked lips.

"You are to be tried in five months time. Till then I suggest you attempt to find some form of contrition."

He nodded in false terror. "Oh, my lady, I am shaking in my boots. Please have mercy." He laughed again, then spit at Katy. It landed on her cheek and ran down to her scar. "I shall look forward to it," he sneered.

She turned and walked toward the exit, spit still running down her face. Degrit released her hand and walked back to the cell. He reached through the bars and caught Thaddeus by the gown. He jerked hard, and Thaddeus' head pounded into the bars.

"You will not ever talk to her like that again. And if you ever spit at her or her sister I will cut your tongue out. Do you understand?" Degrit talked through clenched teeth. Thaddeus nodded dumbly. Degrit pushed him away while still holding tight to his gown then jerked him forward again. His head pounded against the bars a second time.

Degrit left him on the ground holding his head with both hands. He found Katy just outside the door. She was wiping her face with his handkerchief. Her hand shook, and her eyes were full of tears. He took her hand and led her back out into the sunlight.

CHAPTER 24

THE weeks passed quickly. It was such a busy time for everyone in the palace. Degrit and Katy tried to find time to sneak away and be together, but the moments were few and far between.

It was three weeks till the coronation. Waith asked Katy and Eisley to meet with him. When they were all seated in the large parlor, Waith began.

"Your Majesties, I have been so privileged to have served here in the palace. I have watched you both grow up, and I've served under the most noble Queen Wonderland has ever seen. I trust that you will both make me and your mother proud, but..." he took a deep breath, "I am growing older every day. I think it is time for me to retire."

Katy and Eisley both let out sounds of surprise.

"How will we make it without you?" Katy asked.

"You know all you need to know now, Miss Katy. You have all you need to rule this kingdom. And you, too, Eisley. Together you will be a greater force than even your mother. I have a small cottage not far from the palace, and if you have great need of me I can be here very quickly. I shall stay in this role until after Thaddeus' trial, and then I will take a much needed rest."

Katy felt some comfort in the fact that he would be there for the coronation and the trial, but it just felt so strange to think of life at the palace without him. He had been the very first creature in Wonderland she had encountered. He was a part of her life. He was the wisdom and kindness she hoped she could someday attain.

"Waith, we will, of course, support you in your decision, but your absence will create a great hole, and we will miss you very much indeed," Eisley said.

"Yes, we will," Katy agreed. He smiled and bowed low to each of them.

"Thank you, Your Majesties." He slithered out of the room, and Katy felt a piece of what little confidence she had go with him.

* * *

Degrit surprised Katy at the palace later that day. He was in a hurry to go to their place in the woods. They practically ran.

He made sure she was seated comfortably on the little bench, then brought a package out of his jacket. He handed it to her without a word. She tore the paper open. Inside was a tiara made of silver. It was a ring of silver ivy growing around two hearts, made of bloodwood, in the middle. It was elegant and beautiful.

"This is the most beautiful thing I've ever seen." She found it difficult to find words.

"The two hearts represent you and me. And you being the Queen of Hearts, I thought it would be appropriate." He looked nervous.

"Did you make this?" Katy asked in disbelief.

"Yes, but it has to be our secret."

"You're an artist," Katy whispered. She remembered all that she had learned about artists. They were more revered even than royalty, extremely rare in Wonderland, and forbidden to marry.

Degrit ignored the statement and went on rambling about the crown. "I figured that Eisley would wear your mother's crown. So, I...I knew you would need one. Just don't tell anyone where you got it." He fidgeted around like a little boy at his first recital.

"Degrit...this is amazing. I don't know what to say. It's so beautiful, I've never seen anything like it." She stopped, searching for words. "How long have you been hiding this? I mean the fact that you are an artist."

He sighed softly, "I've always created from the time I was young. It's something I have to do, or I feel like I'll explode. My mother always thought I'd be an artist, but it was unclear when I was young and I hadn't yet developed my skill. When you came into the woods that first night, I loved you, and I knew that if I did have the gift I would have to hide it well if I wanted to be with you. I know I shouldn't have made this for you, but I couldn't help it. I just wanted to give you something beautiful to show you that you're ready for this."

Katy felt a fear she had not encountered before, a fear of losing Degrit. She gripped his hand hard. "You took a great risk making this for me. Thank you. I love you." He took the crown out of her hand and placed it on her head. It was perfect. It looked as though silver vines were growing from beneath her black locks. "You can give it to Waith, and after your coronation you can wear it everyday. I hope you'll feel my love when you wear it. Just don't say where it came from," he said.

She nodded and smiled, while a new fear gnawed at her insides.

CHAPTER 25

THE day of the coronation arrived. Katy and Eisley spent the morning in a room being dressed and primped and made up. Katy felt calm, much calmer than she had been before the wedding. Degrit and Waith had been by briefly before rushing off to make sure everything was ready.

Katy wore a long red dress with black laces up the back. Eisley was dressed in a pastel blue that was covered in something sparkly. She looked almost like she was wearing snowflakes.

They were picked up in a carriage pulled by stags. They watched out the windows as they pulled away from the palace and along the path to the Vast Meadowlands.

"Everything is about to change," Eisley said. Katy patted her hand.

"We'll be fine. We'll have each other." Eisley smiled wide and embraced her.

"Indeed," she answered.

They pulled out of the forest, and a deafening sound of cheers came through the windows of the carriage. They peeked out. The meadow was crowded with every kind of creature. There were colorful streamers hanging in various places. A large stage had been set up in the center of the meadow. On the stage were two thrones, each with a banner above it. One read "Eisley, the White Queen," the other, "Katy, the Queen of Hearts."

The carriage pulled slowly through the crowd and made its way to the stage. When Katy and Eisley stepped out of the carriage, a new wave of cheers erupted. The sisters smiled and waved. Waith was next to a podium at the front of the stage. He smiled at them both.

It took several minutes to calm the crowd enough for Waith to speak.

"Ladies and gentlecreatures, we are gathered today for a momentous occasion. This day shall be celebrated for years to come as the day that Wonderland became the land of two queens. Eisley, the White Queen," — there was thunderous applause as Waith pointed his tail toward Eisley, — "and Katy, the Queen of Hearts." He pointed toward Katy now and the crowd responded again.

Waith finished his speech and made sure that the princesses were seated comfortably on their thrones. They sat through songs and poems and speeches. Creatures of all sorts came to the stage to honor them.

At last, the time came for the crowning. Waith approached Eisley first.

"Miss Eisley, please kneel." She stood and adjusted her dress, then knelt in front of Waith. "Eisley, we find you worthy to be our queen. You are kind and compassionate. You are strong and steadfast. You are the daughter of the most noble of Queens. We therefore declare you to be no longer a princess, but as of this moment, Eisley, the White Queen. Long may your rule last," Waith said. Lutwidge lifted her mother's crown onto her head. Waith blinked back tears. The crowd broke into cheers again. Eisley waved graciously. When the cheers began to subside she took her seat again.

Waith made his way over to Katy. "Miss Katy, please kneel." Katy did so. She felt her knees shaking. "Katy, we find you worthy to be our queen. You are wise and true. You are strong and unyielding. You are the daughter of the most noble of Queens. We therefore declare you to be no longer a princess, but as of this moment, Katy, the Queen of Hearts. Long may your rule last," Waith declared. Lutwidge lifted the crown from the box that Katy had stored it in. The crowd gasped at its beauty as Lutwidge lifted it onto Katy's head. Cheers broke out again, and Katy scanned the crowd for Degrit as she waved to her subjects.

She spotted him standing to the left of the stage. He smiled wide and winked at her when their eyes met. She steadied her breathing and waited for the crowd to quiet before she allowed herself to sit.

Eisley looked over at Katy. Their eyes met, and they could see in each other the excitement and the heavy weight of responsibility. Katy hoped that they would make their mother proud. She liked to think that the Queen was watching over them, that she would whisper to them when they were in need of wisdom and guidance.

Shortly after they were crowned, the new Queens were led back to the carriage and taken to the palace. The rest of the kingdom stayed in the meadow and enjoyed celebrating until darkness fell. When the night was black and only a sliver of the moon could be seen, fireworks filled the sky and reminded Katy of that first night with Degrit and the fleets. She didn't know what was ahead, but she held tight to the magic of that moment.

CHAPTER 26

THE celebration of the crowning of the two Queens was set to last three days. There was plenty of merriment to go around. Dancing and singing and performances went on throughout the day. The kingdom had all but forgotten their tragic loss. Joy bubbled from every corner of the meadow.

Katy and Eisley sat under a special tent that Degrit had built for the occasion. They could see all the goings-on without sitting in the hot sun all day. They had a glorious buffet of food, including purple glots brought by none other than Flucial himself. He had decided to like Katy and was much friendlier than the last time they'd met.

They had their choice of drink. Eisley enjoyed drinking the fiddle tree wine (a wine that would cause the drinker to sing her conversation). Katy didn't dare drink it, for fear her horrible singing voice would escape before she could stop it. She was fond of a drink called chendra. It was sweet and tasted a little of black currant, but was actually made from a flower that grew wild and caused a mild intoxication. She felt giddy and bubbly when she drank it. Some of the weight of the crown seemed to lift.

Creatures had been on and off the stage all day, honoring the queens or performing for the crowds entertainment.

Katy was laughing with a skinny lizard Lutwidge had introduced her to. Lutwidge fancied her, and Katy couldn't help but notice the way she grew shy and her scales turned rosy when he was near.

The crowd grew quiet after a man on stage cleared his throat to gain their attention. Katy looked up at him. It was Tomas, Degrit's father. Katy looked over at Degrit with confusion. He shrugged his shoulders.

Tomas stood nervously, wringing his hat in his hands.

"I, uh, well, as many of you know, I lost my dear wife a few years ago," he began. "Since then, I, well, I haven't been the best father to my son. I haven't had much left to give him. But I want to change. I want to do something for him. Something that will, well, better his life. So, I am here today on this stage to announce that my son, Degrit...is an artist."

The crowd went wild with sounds of shock and loud whispers. Katy's heart dropped into her stomach, and Degrit grabbed onto the chair nearest him. Tomas cleared his throat again.

"He is too modest and would never take credit, but I, well, I saw him making that crown there, for the Queen," he pointed his finger at Katy. As the crowd turned to look at it again, Katy reminded her face to smile.

Tomas had his failings for certain, but he was renowned for being an honest man. It took no more than his word, and the kingdom was in a frenzy of excitement. Degrit was herded onto the stage. Standing suddenly next to his well-meaning father. Degrit's mouth smiled, while his eyes were welling with sorrow.

Eisley grabbed Katy's hand and looked into her eyes. Her expression was of shock and horror. Katy was confused and felt as though the chendra drained out of her, along with every good feeling she'd ever had.

Degrit stood on stage to thunderous applause and shook his father's hand. A celebratory dance broke out among all the creatures, and Degrit took that moment to slip away. The creatures around him patted him on the back and shook his hand vigorously. He pushed his way out of the crowd and ran toward the forest.

"Katy, did Degrit really make that for you?" Eisley asked.

Katy nodded. "I have to find him," she gasped. Eisley nodded.

"Lutwidge, take Katy to Degrit. He ran toward the forest," Eisley commanded. Lutwidge nodded and cleared a path for him and Katy in the right direction.

As she followed Lutwidge, Katy felt that her chest might explode. Pain and fear were growing in her gut. As they neared the palace, Katy saw Degrit on the bench in the woods. He was bent over with his head in both hands, and she could see that he was sobbing.

She thanked Lutwidge and ran toward Degrit. Despair wrapped itself around her heart and squeezed so hard that it was difficult to breathe.

Katy inhaled deeply and walked toward Degrit. The closer she got, the further away she felt.

"Degrit," she whispered. He didn't look up when she spoke.

"Why, Katy? Why is this happening? How could I be so stupid," he spoke with a shaky voice.

"Degrit, you're not stupid! I don't know! Oh, God, Degrit, I'm so sorry!! How can we fix this?" She knelt next to him, and tears started filling her eyes.

"We can't, Katy. We can't. I know that my dad was trying to do something good for me, but..." He looked up at her for the first time.

Tears were streaming down his face. Katy knelt in front of him and put her hands on his knees.

"So what do we do now?" she asked through her tears.

"I don't know what we can do." He put his head down again.

"Isn't there something? I mean, can't I change the law? I am the Queen." He looked up at her.

"Katy, this isn't just a law. It's foundational to our society. Artists are on a different plane than the rest of the kingdom. It's supposed to be a great honor to give your life up to bring beauty to the kingdom. I don't have a choice in this, and neither do you," he said. "Do you think your subjects would accept a Queen who marries one of their beloved artists? Someone they believe should dedicate their lives to creating art for them? I can't let you risk your throne for me," he said.

"I don't care. I don't want the throne. I want you! We have to try. There has to be a way!" she said.

He looked up at her and smiled sadly. "Katy, I would rather love you and live in a hole in the ground with the billdralls than be an artist and live without you. I don't care about the honor and glory. All I want is you." He held her face in both his hands.

"We'll make it work. We'll find a way." Katy spoke with desperation in her voice.

He shook his head in disbelief. "I won't give up without a fight, my love. But I have little faith that we will win this battle," he said.

She held his hands tightly in hers. "Perhaps we can be the ones to change the course of history," she said. "We must at least try." She clung to hope. She was, after all, the Queen. Surely she would be able to bring a much-needed change to tradition. She didn't know what kind of fight she would be up against, but she knew this was worth fighting for.

CHAPTER 27

KATY didn't return to the meadow that day. Degrit went to talk to his father, to thank him, and to forgive him in his heart. Katy spent the rest of that day and night curled up on her bed. Eisley came and sat beside her when she returned late in the evening.

"Eisley...is there any hope?" Katy whispered.

Eisley paused for a long time. "I don't know where your path will lead, Katylove. I certainly couldn't see where mine was going to lead me. We seem to be very unlucky in love, sister." She stayed with her for much of the night and tried to bring comfort. The night was long.

* * *

The next day Eisley helped Katy get dressed and ready to greet her subjects. Katy's face was swollen from the crying, so Eisley put ice cold water on cloths and laid them over her face until the swelling went down. When Katy was presentable they loaded into the carriage again and headed toward the meadow. Eisley held Katy's hand.

"Katy, be prepared. Today there will be much talk about Degrit. We have fallen into the shadows in light of this news." Katy nodded. She braced herself for a difficult day.

When they arrived, they were escorted to their tent. They noticed that Degrit was on the stage in a chair. Creatures were lined up in an endless queue to have an opportunity to talk with him. They were bowing and giving gifts and thanking him for what he would do for Wonderland. He looked empty. He smiled graciously and shook their hands, but there was nothing behind his eyes.

Katy saw now what they were up against. Hope began to leak out of her heart. She tried to convince herself that everything was going to work out, but she found herself harder and harder to believe.

When she looked down again, she saw a nervous rabbit standing near the tent entrance, waiting to be let in. Lutwidge let him through but kept a close eye on him, as he acted rather suspiciously.

Katy recognized him immediately. It was Nash. He came near her throne and bowed. He fiddled with his jacket collar, which was worn from all of his nervous moments.

"Your Majesty, I don't know if you will remember me, but I am close friends with Degrit. My name is..."

Before he could finish Katy completed his sentence. "Nash. Of course I remember you. It's a great pleasure to see you again." Katy was glad to see him, but she found it very difficult to put any joy in her tone at the moment.

"Thank you, Your Majesty. I...um...." he glanced over at Eisley, who was very engrossed in a conversation with a caterpillar. He stepped closer to Katy. "I am very concerned about Degrit," he whispered to her. "He is not at all himself. I think this should be the happiest day of his life, but he is miserable. I know he looks happy enough, but I can see right through that. He's all wrong." He pulled one of his ears down and nibbled on the end of it before he spoke again. "I came to you because I know you are very close, and I thought maybe you could help," he said.

"Nash, I think perhaps you should talk with him. He probably needs a good friend now. He has quite a few new situations to handle. You are just the rabbit to help him walk through those," Katy said. Nash stood straight and pulled his shoulders back a bit with pride. Katy didn't want to talk about Degrit right now, but she felt such compassion for this nervous little bunny that she had to humor him.

"But Your Majesty, I know nothing about all these situations. How could I possibly help him?" He held his ear close to his mouth and nibbled at the end now and then.

"Perhaps what he needs most right now is someone to listen. And as I remember, you are a very good listener," Katy assured him.

He stopped for a moment and considered what she'd said. "Yes, ma'am. You know, I think you're right. He does need a friend, and I might not be able to offer helpful advice, but I can listen. Thank you, Your Majesty." He bowed several times, then headed out of the tent.

Katy didn't allow herself to think about Degrit for long. She had to push that aside. She had a special compartment in her heart for things that needed to be dealt with later. For now, she was the Queen of Hearts, and she didn't feel pain or hurt.

CHAPTER 28

THE festival was finally over. The banners and confetti were being cleaned up by a hardworking crew of creatures hired just for the celebration. The meadow looked as though a rainbow had exploded over it.

Katy and Eisley were back at the palace getting settled as new Queens. Waith remained there with them for the time, and Katy was grateful for his presence. He had a way of making her believe she was worthy of this crown and could actually run the kingdom.

The morning after the party, Degrit and Katy asked to meet with him. They met in a private parlor with a small round table surrounded by tall yellow chairs. They gathered around the tight little circle the table created, seating themselves in the chairs.

After they had all spoken their hellos, Katy glanced at Degrit. His face was swollen, and his eyes were vacant. He caught her gaze and nodded that he would begin the conversation.

"Waith, you always seem to be one step ahead in everything, so you may be aware of why we are here." He paused to give Waith a moment to respond. Waith gave no sign that he understood. "Well, you know it has been discovered that I am an artist...." As he said this, Katy felt a knife in her heart.

Waith jumped in, as though he had just been cued, "Oh yes, of course, we are all very excited! Congratulations." He patted Degrit on the back with the tip of his tail. Degrit sighed deeply and plodded ahead.

"Thank you, but, Waith, Katy and I...well...we are in love. We want to spend our lives together. We hoped to marry someday...." As Degrit trailed off, Waith suddenly sat up straighter and looked intently at Degrit.

"What are you saying?" Waith was shocked.

"We want to get married," Katy cut in.

"Absolutely not. You cannot speak like this! You will be ended if you continue with these absurd ideas. What are you — "

"Surely you knew that we were in love!" Katy interrupted. Waith looked at her sternly.

"Yes, of course, Your Majesty. But now you must put all that behind you. Do you have any idea what the consequences of even speaking about this would be?" he said.

"Put it behind us?!" Katy spoke louder than she intended. She stood and paced as Waith continued. He sighed heavily and looked at Katy with compassion.

"Miss Katy, I understand how you must feel. You may not know this, but I was once in love. Her name was Heleena. She was killed by a bandersnatch. I know how it feels to lose someone who holds the other half of your heart." His eyes had misted over and he was gazing into the distance, looking into a memory he was reluctant to return from. "But this is not something to be toyed with. This idea, this desire, has got to go. It could destroy you both. It could destroy the kingdom.

It cannot happen! It cannot ever be mentioned again." He stared intently into Degrit's eyes. "Degrit, if you truly love her, you must get these ideas out of your head. You must leave her. If there had been a way I could have saved Heleena, I would have done it, even if it meant I would never be with her again. You know what they will do to her. They would hate her for trying to steal away an artist! If you love her, Let. Her. Go."

"No! No!" Katy felt all the emotions she had been feebly holding back come rushing into her like a wave hitting her full force. Anger was the first on the scene. "No, why are saying this, Waith? I thought you cared about us! Why are you doing this?" She stood over him.

He tilted his head in concern. "My dear Katy, it is *because* I love you that I say this. I know that you were not born in Wonderland, and part of your education here was missed in some degrees. It must be very difficult for you to understand. It must even seem harsh to you, but you must try to understand. An artist here is like a god. The kingdom expects him to give up everything and serve them. They would do the same if they were discovered to be an artist. They would leave everything they love to bring beauty to us all. It is the way of our world," he said.

Katy looked imploringly at Degrit. He wouldn't look at her. Waith looked back and forth between the two of them.

"I will be happy to help you both in any way I can, but I cannot entertain this idea. I cannot be a part of something that would be the death of you." He slithered off his chair. He looked back at them from the door. "Please, don't speak this to another soul. The next may not be as kind," he said.

Katy shot daggers at him with her eyes. She slammed the door behind him.

"I cannot believe him!! I thought for certain he would be on our side," she spat the words out. Degrit was at the table with his head in his hands. He didn't look up.

"He is on our side, and he's right," he whispered.

Katy felt heat travel through her body. "What do you mean?" She trembled all over.

Now he looked at her. His eyes were dry and emotionless. "Katy, we can't do this. Waith loves us both and look at his reaction. Imagine how all the other creatures in the kingdom would react. I love you too much to put your life and future in danger." A thin stream of tears began to push its way out of his eyes.

"I thought you said you would fight," Katy accused in a softer voice.

"Katy, I can do no wrong to them. They think I am practically a savior. If I 'fight,' I will be throwing you to the lions. I'll be innocent in their eyes. They will despise and destroy you. And as Thaddeus proved, there is evil in this world. I can't bear the thought of you tasting the same fate as your mother. This isn't a fair fight, Katy. I won't sacrifice you just so I can have you." He leaned his head on the back of the chair.

"How, but...how...how can we do this? How can we just give up?" She couldn't stop the streams of tears coming from her own eyes.

"I'm not ever going to stop loving you, Raven. I'm not ever going to give up on that. We are out of options. We can't run away. Who here has not seen our faces? There is nowhere that isolated. There are creatures all over the countryside, and our whereabouts would be announced in hours. We can't come out and say that we want to get married. No, that would be suicidal." He paused for a moment. "Meet me in the meadow tonight. We'll say goodbye." He stood abruptly and left the room.

Katy collapsed and gave herself over to sorrow.

CHAPTER 29

As Katy walked toward the meadow in the dark of evening, she felt she was walking to her death. She knew that part of her heart would die after this night. She put on a simple white dress and wore no shoes. She took her black hair down and let it blow with the wind. This was the last time she would be allowed out dressed in such a way. She left the beautiful, — but now tainted, —crown on her dresser.

The warm breeze felt all wrong. She wanted a storm or a strong wind that brought fear and terror, but the evening was perfect. As she stepped into the meadow, she saw that Degrit was dressed nearly exactly as he had been that very first night.

The fleets were out and hovering all around the meadow. Katy sucked in her breath at the strength of the emotion the memory of that first night carried with it.

Degrit walked to her and took her hand. They walked slowly, carefully, not wanting to set the fleets into motion. There was a blanket spread in the soft grass. They sat next to each other, and Katy felt the trembling return. They sat there with their hands clutching each other, sitting as close as they could manage. There was silence for a long time.

"Katy, I don't know how to do this. How do you say goodbye to someone who is intertwined with your own soul?" He gathered her up in a tight embrace. They cried together.

"This is the hardest thing I've ever done," Katy said. "You were there for me when my mother died...." She tried to gain control of her breathing before she spoke again. "How am I going to survive losing you without you there to hold me together?"

"I don't think this is a wound that will ever really heal. If we ever try to let it, it will be ripped open when we see each other again. If I had known that my fate would contain living with such pain, I might have ended it all long ago. Now I can't bear to leave without you," he spoke with deep regret. "This is our last chance to be 'us.' I just want to hold you and hope this feeling of you next to me will stay with me for the rest of my days." He closed his eyes and pulled her closer. She breathed in his smell. She didn't want to forget anything, didn't want to lose an ounce of what was him.

They cried there together until their sobs slowed to deep, heavy breaths. They were lying on the blanket looking into each other's eyes. Degrit was stroking Katy's hair. She ran her fingers along his face, memorizing every inch. He had little lines beside his eyes that only appeared when he smiled. She loved them. She longed to see them again.

Katy stood up and held out her hand. "I think it's time to get these fleets moving," she said. He took her hand and stood beside her.

"On three," he said. "One, two, three..." Before he even got the words out, Katy was running wild through the meadow yelling at the top of her lungs. It felt so good to have a release, to let the feelings out in the form of a scream. The fleets shot off in all directions, leaving trails of light. Katy spun to look at Degrit and together they ran through the lights till they were covered head to toe in every imaginable color. They glowed like some sort of supernatural beings. When they looked at each other, they burst into laughter and collapsed in the grass. They laughed until their sides ached. Katy touched the laugh lines near Degrit's eyes and committed them to memory.

The fleets' trails were visible long after the fleets were gone. Katy hoped their love would be the same.

"I'm leaving in the morning," Degrit said. His face was serious again. "My village has prepared a cottage for Nash and me. He's been worried about me. I asked if he would be my assistant. I thought it might be good to have some company." He smiled weakly. "I'll stay away from the palace as much as I can. I think it will be easier for both of us." He squeezed Katy's hand.

"What will I do?" Katy asked in a whisper.

"You will become the greatest queen that Wonderland has ever had. You'll be strong, and you'll be the Katy who has shown me what it is to love someone with all that you are," he said.

Neither of them wanted to leave. They wanted the night to hang on longer. They both felt the pain of the first rays of sunlight. They held hands till they reached the palace, then stood at the door made beautiful by the last artist. To Katy it was an ugly symbol of something she had to shut out. Degrit grabbed her face in both hands and looked into her eyes intently.

"Do not ever think that this was a dream, or that I don't love you anymore. I will be loving you with all my heart with every breath I ever take. I love you, Katy. I consider myself lucky to have held your heart for the short time that I did." He kissed her and pulled her tight against him. "I love you, darling," he said as he pulled away.

"I love you, too," she said. "You'll always hold my heart."

"Goodbye," he said. The word felt like poison. They both felt it, and it made walking away harder. She watched him walk into the forest and out of her life, but not out of her heart.

CHAPTER 30

KATY could not allow herself to become the weeping, emotional mess that she wanted to become. She was attempting to rule a kingdom. She built a wall, a thick, heavy wall around her heart. Most of the creatures in the palace had no knowledge of what had happened, and they were never suspicious. Katy carried herself as a queen, elegant and emotionless.

Eisley worried about her and tried to talk with Katy, but once the goodbyes were said, Katy didn't want to open the wound again. The two Queens spent some of their time together, but most of their duties took them separate ways. It gave them the advantage of being two places at once.

Katy was usually in charge of open court, when subjects could come in to voice complaints or make requests. But Eisley liked to be involved when she had the time.

On this particular day, Eisley and Katy sat next to each other in twin thrones. They had been sitting for nearly three hours, listening to subjects and giving medals or settling arguments.

An elephant was stepping aside after he had been thanked for all his help in building a community school. Katy was looking into the crowd, wondering how long this day would last, when she heard Eisley speaking to someone. Cheshire had made himself at home on Eisley's lap, purring affectionately. He seemed to have bonded with Eisley in a deeper way than anyone could bond with Katy now.

"Nash, isn't it? How lovely to see you. You look very dashing. What an incredible hat. Wherever did you get it?" Eisley asked. Katy looked up to see Nash with the hat now removed from his head and being held in his fidgeting paws.

"Degrit made it for me," he answered.

Eisley nodded. "Of course," she said.

Nash shifted his gaze toward Katy. "Your Majesty, I was wondering if I might be so bold as to approach the throne?"

"Of course, Nash," Katy answered. He stepped forward cautiously, as though at any moment the Queen might change her mind. When he stood just feet away from Katy, he leaned forward.

"Your Majesty, I just wanted to make you personally aware of a situation, to see if you have any wisdom to offer. As you know, I am living with Degrit now." It hurt Katy every time the name was spoken. "I have been feeling rather strange lately, having lots of vivid happy memories, but also finding it difficult to think straight. To cut this all short, I discovered that Degrit has been growing danglias inside our cottage. You are familiar with these flowers aren't you, Your Majesty?"

"Yes, Degrit introduced them to me," she answered.

"I don't mean to speak ill of him. I'm just concerned and thought perhaps you would want to come talk to him. I know you're friends." Nash turned the hat over and over in his paws.

Eisley reached over and touched Katy's arm.

"Katy, go if you need to. I can handle the rest of the subjects." Katy nodded gratefully and headed to the stables to get Fleetfoot. Nash hopped close behind her.

"Can you ride?" she asked Nash.

"No ma'am, I'm a bit too nervous for horses, but you go on. I will be there as soon as I can." Katy smiled at him and gave Fleetfoot a gentle kick.

* * *

Katy found the cottage right where Nash had described. It was small and fairly isolated. There was a stream running past, clear water rushing over smooth stones. Large fiddle trees surrounded the land. It was the perfect place for an artist to work.

She tied Fleetfoot to a nearby tree next to the stream. She knocked lightly on the door, and when no one answered, she knocked again harder. She pushed the door open after a few moments and found Degrit standing near a window, eyes closed, breathing deeply. She looked just below him to a group of danglias thriving in a window box. She ripped the flowers up and threw them out the front door.

Degrit smiled and took another deep breath. His eyes remained closed. Katy grabbed him by the shoulders and shook him hard. His eyes came open, but they were clouded and dark.

"Why is a raven like a writing desk?" he asked. His expression was sad and concerned. He was looking for something he'd lost.

Katy felt hot tears running down her face. "Degrit, it's me. I am your Raven, remember? You said I was like a writing desk you could pour your heart out on. Remember!! Degrit, snap out of it!!" She was shouting and shaking him.

At last he shook his head and blinked several times. His eyes remained cloudy.

"Katy?" He looked at her suspiciously, unsure if she was real. She nodded, and he grabbed her in a tight embrace. "Katy!!" He held her tight. She pulled away and looked intently into his face.

"Degrit, what are you doing?" She pointed toward the now empty window box where she had ripped out the danglias. His hands were touching her face and running through her hair. He stopped at her words and his shoulders sagged. He sank into the chair behind him.

"It's more difficult than I'd imagined. I can't seem to convince my mind that I must let go of you; it's intent on thinking about you all the time. It hurt so bad. I just thought that if I must be here in this little cabin without you that I could, at least, relive some of my moments with you. So what if I lose some of my sanity? Who am I keeping it for anyway?" He stared at her, afraid she might vanish. She could see him there hiding behind the clouds in his eyes.

"Degrit, I can't bear to see you this way. Please! I don't want to lose you completely. You are stronger than this." Katy felt the tears running down her neck and into the collar of her dress. She wiped at them and then sank into the seat across from him. Degrit leaned forward and touched her face again. He stared for a long time.

"Katy...I...I'll try, but I'm not strong like you. The pain sits on top of me, and I just can't breathe or move. I'm paralyzed. The memories lift the pain enough for me to create, to move again." He got up suddenly and went over to an open area full of windows. There were several tables of various heights holding different projects in all stages of completion.

There were paintings and sketches, but the recurring theme seemed to be hats. They were beautiful and unique, all sizes and shapes, all styles and colors.

"Look," he said, as he held his hands out to display all his work. His eyes had changed. They were vacant and crazed. He stepped from table to table picking up his creations and dancing around the room with them. "I made her a hat, a crown, a hat and that's how it all started. If I make another one, a better one...maybe I can fix things. Maybe things will be the way they were." He was different. Frantic and distant. She wondered how long he had been breathing in the plant's toxins.

"They are amazing," she said. New tears came for what she could see had already been lost. Her Degrit had gone. A portion of him was left, but she knew now that the night in the meadow had been more of a goodbye than she had realized.

His face dropped again, and his eyes grew dark. "She'll be angry with me. My raven. She won't like the flowers. She won't want me to have them." Katy rose and walked to him. She took his hands in hers.

"My dearest, Degrit, I am your Raven. It's me. I'm not angry. I am heartbroken," she said.

"I know that you are my Raven. Of course you are. I love you, Katy." He spun around, then held a finger up to represent a brilliant idea. "Come with me. You must see the stream." He took her hand and nearly ran to the stream outside the cottage. He patted his hand on a little bench next to it. "Here you are, my dear. Please sit."

She sat next to him on the bench. He sat with his arm around her, and she leaned her head into him. She pretended he had not left her. When she looked closer at this stream that he loved so much, she saw that patches of danglia had been planted everywhere. He had done the job thoroughly. When he spoke again his voice sounded different.

"Katy." The tone startled her. She looked up at his face. She could see him there again, the boy she loved.

"Degrit!" His eyes were clear and pooling with tears, but not the depressed and manic tears she had seen earlier.

"I'm sorry," he said. "I wasn't as strong as I thought." She wanted to stay here in this moment. She wanted him to stay with her. He kissed the top of her head and stroked her black hair. And then the moment flew away and with it went the part of Degrit that was still Degrit.

He suddenly jumped up. "How rude I am. I didn't even introduce myself." Katy shook his hand and went through several inane introductions, including being introduced to several trees, the stream, and some of the hats he had created.

She walked toward Fleetfoot, knowing that Degrit had now truly left her. She was angry and hurt and felt abandoned. She used those feelings as mortar to make the wall around her heart stronger.

She met Nash on her way out. She advised him to leave Degrit if he valued his sanity. Somehow, though, she knew that he valued Degrit more than sanity, and she understood why.

CHAPTER 31

KATY sat at her window every morning, giving herself just a moment to drink her tea and enjoy some silence before the busyness of the royal life began. It was quiet. The sun was peeking out from above the trees, and the sky was a brilliant shade of purple.

These contemplative moments were the only ones she allowed herself. The emotions she was burying alive within dark walls were allowed their say for just a moment in the first morning light.

She let her thoughts stray to Degrit. It was always the first place they wanted to go. But after yesterday's visit to his cottage, the thoughts had changed. Sorrow still reigned, and she still missed him more than words would contain, but a new darkness grew. She knew this one. She had encountered it before. It had come just after her mother's death. Degrit had been the one to help her fight it off, but he was gone. He was really gone. And now, without him here to fight it off, a deep hatred began to take root in her chest. It wrapped its stringy tendrils around the walls and laced its way into the fleshy parts of her heart.

The logical part of her knew that what happened with Degrit wasn't her fault. But some angry emotional demon in her soul kept shooting accusations at her, making her feel that somehow she was responsible for all the heartache, that if she could just be different or better she wouldn't find everyone around her getting hurt. She hadn't been able to stop her mother's death. She hadn't been able to save Degrit. She wasn't really supposed to be a queen. She was an impostor. She hated the Queen of Hearts. She hated the Raven. She covered the mirror in her room with a blood red cloth.

This was the favorite playground of her mind. She could spend all morning bathing in this hatred.

The sun finally exploded over the trees in a rich gold color, and Katy closed the walls of her own heart again and set about to the work of being Queen.

CHAPTER 32

KATY noticed Eisley's discomfort. They were both at breakfast. Waith was sitting across the table from them. Katy had forgiven Waith. Her love and respect for him went too deep and she couldn't bear losing him, too.

Cheshire was curled up in Eisley's lap again. He would hardly look at Katy anymore. He had chosen loyalty to the White Queen. She stroked him nervously now, and her eyes had a strange sorrow behind them.

"Are you all right, Your Majesty?" Waith asked Eisley.

"Hmmm? Oh, yes, just a bit nervous about today, you know?" Her food sat untouched. Thaddeus was to be tried today.

Trials were held in a special courtroom. They were not held in the throne room, and Katy was grateful. The last time she had seen Thaddeus in that room, he had been slicing her mother's throat and giving her a slender scar along her jawline. She began to brace herself for the proceedings. She still felt uncertain about her emotion and how she would respond.

Waith gave them an encouraging speech about how much faith he had in them and how he knew they would make the best decision for the kingdom. But as Eisley glanced up at Katy, they were both certain of only one thing, and that was each other's uncertainty.

* * *

The courtroom was full when Eisley and Katy arrived and settled themselves in their box, perched slightly above the proceedings. They looked out over the crowd and saw a pair of guards dragging in a reluctant Thaddeus. His feet were trailing behind him, and his head hung down toward the floor.

Katy took a deep breath. Eisley's eyes were wide and already threatening to fill with tears. Katy took her hand and squeezed it, encouraging her sister to be strong. Eisley attempted to smile.

Lutwidge stood and began reading off the charges and announcing the case. Katy smiled to herself. Lutwidge had become so different — still the same kindness and grace, but hardly a stammer was left. He spoke with almost no trace of the difficulty he used to have. Katy could see how the crowd looked at him and realized that he had become quite a hero in the kingdom.

Lutwidge bowed and stepped back. The guards dragged Thaddeus to the front. He stood on his own. He was only feet away from them. At last he lifted his head, and his eyes met Eisley's. She caught her breath.

His face was different than it had been in the prison cell. Katy saw the play he was making and became even angrier. Tears were streaming down his face. He was the picture of repentance and sorrow. He looked at Eisley the way he had looked at her when she had visited his village so long ago.

He fell to his knees, then spoke. Even his tone felt slippery and manipulative to Katy.

"My love, you are as beautiful as ever. I have spent these last long months thinking of nothing but you. How can I ever make things right? How can I be sorry enough for what has happened?"

Katy glanced over at Eisley. Tears were streaming down her cheeks, and she looked at him with love and forgiveness. Katy let out an angry breath and rolled her eyes.

"What's *happened*?? What's *happened*? Thaddeus, you will be silent until I give you permission to speak," she shouted. Thaddeus made eye contact with Katy now and she could see the venom was still there beneath the surface. "Thaddeus, *what has happened* is that you brutally murdered our mother and attempted to do the same to me. You say it as though you had nothing to do with it. You have very little hope of convincing me otherwise, since I still bear the scar!" He bowed his head toward the ground and sobbed. Katy continued, "Now I will give you a moment to speak your story, to tell me why you should receive any mercy from me. But tread carefully, or you will lose your speaking privileges altogether."

He nodded. He turned his head and eyes back to Eisley as he spoke. Katy bit her tongue and let him speak. This had to be a fair trial. She had to let him make his plea.

"Your Majesty, I was poisoned with thicnia. The bear and his brothers, they hated the Queen and wanted to overthrow her. They needed a way in, though. When they found out that I was to be married to you, they poisoned my food with thicnia." Katy knew about thicnia. Waith had educated her on it several years ago. He told her it's a toxin that works almost like hypnosis. Someone can poison you and then tell you what they want you to do, and it will stay in your mind like a command until that deed is done. Thaddeus continued, always keeping his focus on Eisley. "They told me to marry you and kill the Queen. I loved your mother. I would never want to kill her, and I would NEVER want to hurt you. I was under their spell. Please have mercy on me, my love."

Katy stood. "ENOUGH!" she shouted. Eisley looked up at her in shock.

"Katy, what are you doing?" she whispered. Katy sat back in her chair and continued.

"Thaddeus, you are found guilty of plotting, planning, and executing the murder of the Queen. You may be able to make others in this room believe you, but you must remember that I WAS THERE! That bear was a mindless servant of yours. You were the ringleader. It was your knife and your hand that killed my mother and tried to end me. You were under no spell except the spell that your black heart casts on your mind. You will speak no further today, sir." Katy was surprised by how full of authority her voice was.

Thaddeus glared at her and then shifted his gaze once again to Eisley. The sad, love-struck eyes did their work on her sister. Eisley leaned over to Katy.

"Katy, please, what are you going to do? Please have mercy on him," Eisley whispered. Katy felt something rise up in her. It was unlike anything she had ever felt, a force more powerful than she was. She stood again and pointed at Thaddeus.

"Thaddeus, I have heard quite enough of your lies. You have no good in you. You are sentenced to DEATH!" She heard a gasp from her sister and felt her clutching at her dress trying to stop her, but Katy would not be stopped. She looked at the guards as she made her next command. "OFF WITH HIS HEAD!"

"No...." Eisley whispered. She began to cry.

"Eisley, my love, please, don't let her kill me. I love you, Eisley. Please, have mercy. I was tricked. Please forgive me. Have mercy, please love..." Thaddeus kept at it even when he was out of the courtroom and they could barely hear his cries. The crowd filed outside to watch the execution.

Lutwidge approached the Queens. He bowed low. "Your Majesties...w-would either of you like to attend the execution or sh-should we proceed without you?" he asked.

Katy shook her head. "Proceed," she said. He nodded and headed outside to give the order.

The room cleared. Katy sat staring ahead, breathing hard. Eisley was sobbing quietly next to her. They could hear Lutwidge give the order, and Thaddeus was still pleading and shouting his love. A loud WHACK sounded, and Thaddeus was forever silenced. Eisley fell to the floor and sobbed hard and loud. Katy tried to comfort her, but quickly realized that she would not be able to give her any comfort. She left her there with her maids.

Katy walked out of the courtroom, her jaw set and her eyes empty. She saw Waith slithering away out of the corner of her vision. She walked into the throne room and sat in the throne that had once been her mother's. She had made a hard decision today, one that hurt her sister, but she knew that she was absolutely right about Thaddeus. She felt power and anger coursing through her veins. She hated the Queen of Hearts. *The Queen of Hearts has no heart,* she thought.

CHAPTER 33

AFTER Thaddeus' trial, there was a dark cloud over the palace. Waith had disappeared without a word. Eisley hadn't spoken to Katy. She had locked herself in her room for days without eating. The creatures who worked in the palace were desperately worried about her. Word leaked out to other creatures in the kingdom. The kingdom loved their White Queen. One by one subjects began coming to the palace to leave gifts for Eisley. They left her poems, cards, food, but mostly, they left white roses.

The servants who worked at the palace would carry it all up to her room every day. She refused to come out, so they arranged it all in the sitting room outside her bedroom.

Katy stayed away. She knew that she was the cause of Eisley's pain, and she didn't want to push the knife in any further. The workers in the palace saw this as indifference. Katy noticed that she was treated differently after the trial. She was feared. She hated it. She wanted to be loved as Eisley was. If only they had been there. They would have known that she had done the right thing.

Lutwidge came to her one day as she was sitting in the parlor.

"Your Majesty, may I have a word?" he asked as he peeked into the doorway.

"Yes, of course, please come in, Lutwidge." He came into the room and sat in the chair next to her. She noticed the way he carried himself with such confidence and certainty. He was not the same as he had been. He had lost the parts of himself that contained fear and insecurity.

"Miss Katy, I just w-wanted to tell you that I believe you did the r-right thing. I was there. I witnessed his evil too. Miss Eisley will n-never be able to understand the things we saw. She n-never saw that side of him. I know that your subjects don't understand either, but I w-wanted you to know that I *do* understand, and I think that you m-made the right decision. I'm not sure what will happen now, but I just thought you n-needed someone to support you." He looked at her sympathetically.

"Thank you, Lutwidge. I can't tell you how much it means to hear you say that." He smiled, stood, and bowed.

"I am at your service if ever you n-need me. Also, I have taken the liberty of looking into the story that Thaddeus told. I wanted to be certain that the b-bear had no brothers that might be plotting evil. Apparently, he had been abandoned as a cub and spent most of his life alone. Thaddeus showed him some k-kindness and he willingly went along with him. It seems the threat is dead," he said.

"Thank you so much, Lutwidge. You are most loyal and brave. I am so honored to have you here in the palace," Katy said. Lutwidge smiled, bowed low, and left the room.

Katy sighed. She heard a sound and thought for a moment that he was coming back in. When she looked, she saw what looked like a ghost. It was Eisley. She was paper thin. Her white dress hung loosely on her bony frame. She was pale, and her eyes were lifeless.

"Eisley!" Katy stood and walked to her.

"I heard....I heard your conversation with Lutwidge," Eisley said in a hoarse whisper. "I trust him and you above anyone else."

"Eisley, I am so sorry!" Katy ushered Eisley over to the chair. She looked as though standing was a task that just might be unbearable. She almost fell into the chair.

"Please forgive me. I know this must feel so hurtful," Katy said.

Eisley's breathing was labored. She held her hand up to stop Katy's words.

"Katy, it's I who am sorry. I have barely had time to overcome the sorrow of mother's death. Seeing Thaddeus....hearing his words...I was seduced by his so-called love. As I sat sequestered in my room, I finally gave mother all the tears I had left. Then when I stopped crying for her, I gave some for my groom." Her speaking came in short little bursts as she found the energy and breath to get it out. "It was then that my mind came to rest on my sweet little sister. You, who had to witness our mother being murdered, who had to make a decision to keep our kingdom safe even if it meant hurting someone you love. Katy, you are a good Queen. And after hearing what Lutwidge said, it just confirmed what I came to believe in my room. You did the right thing. I'm sorry that I have made it more difficult."

Katy knelt in front of her and embraced her. She was so frail. Katy didn't squeeze too hard for fear of breaking her.

"Did you see all your love gifts from your subjects?" Katy asked.

"Yes, I love the white roses! They've always been my favorite," she smiled.

"Well, you are the White Queen." Katy said. "They suit you perfectly."

CHAPTER 34

KATY was running the kingdom. Eisley didn't look much better, though she had been out of her room for weeks. She was still ghostly and thin. Her spirits seemed lifted, though. She was out conversing with her subjects for a few hours nearly every day. The creatures in Wonderland adored the White Queen, and they were overjoyed at her recovery.

The castle was filled with white roses. Katy began to wonder how long this would go on. It wasn't slowing down. The kingdom loved Eisley, and the other side of the coin was that they despised Katy. No one would dare speak it or show it, but Katy felt it. She was the reason their precious White Queen had become ill and nearly died. She had caused all the heartache.

Eisley was as kind as ever. She had, however, lost something in her despair. She was a child again in many ways. She wasn't completely insane, but she wasn't completely sane either. She was sweet and forgiving to Katy and gave her no reason to feel anything but love toward her. Katy knew that she would never be loved by her subjects as Eisley was, but while she couldn't pretend it didn't bother her at times, she understood. Eisley was easy to love.

* * *

As Katy walked along the grounds the next day, she heard giggles that were familiar to her. She peeked around the corner to see Eisley laughing with a stranger. Katy's heart was lightened to see her happy again. She was leaning in and talking with the stranger as though they were the best of friends. Katy could only see the man's back. He wore a deep purple velvet suit and a top hat to match. Wild blond hair stuck out in all directions from under the hat. Katy's breath stopped. She leaned in further and heard a voice almost as familiar to her as her own. Degrit! She could see by their behavior that this was not the first meeting. Eisley suddenly spotted her.

"Oh! Katylove! Come join us! We are having great fun with riddles." Eisley smiled and gestured to Katy. Degrit turned to look at her. His face showed no sign of recognition. His eyes were vacant, almost dopey. He smiled wide at her.

Katy politely declined and ran to her room. She knew that Eisley would never do anything to hurt her. But Eisley, did not always remember things that mattered anymore. Katy wondered how long they had been spending time together. Her heart ached from seeing Degrit again, and seeing them laughing together opened a dark place of jealousy in her heart. She knew it was innocent, — they would never be romantic, — but it didn't lessen the pain.

She called Lutwidge to her room and asked him about it. He had a pulse on everything that went on in the palace.

"They have become quite close friends and spend much of their time t-together. They normally meet outside the palace, and I suppose that you have been too b-busy with all your duties to see. They are both very simple spirits now and are very childlike. They sit and t-tell silly jokes or have tea parties for hours." He answered.

"Thank you, Lutwidge," Katy said. As he left, he turned to face her once more.

"Miss Katy, I am certain that Eisley does n-not mean to hurt you. She has lost much of her memory."

"Of course, Lutwidge. Can you get a message to Waith that I would like to meet with him?" Lutwidge nodded and left the room.

Katy could not live in peace with the love of her life galavanting around the courtyard with her sister. It wasn't fair. It hurt every time she saw him or even heard his name, and he felt nothing.

* * *

"Your Majesty, I have a m-message for you," Lutwidge said a few weeks later. He handed her a scroll.

It had been a stressful season. Katy had run into Eisley and Degrit several times since her initial encounter, and it had not become any easier. Every time, it felt like her heart was being ripped out. Katy took the scroll and walked into the parlor to read it in privacy. She recognized Waith's handwriting immediately:

My dear Katy,

Lutwidge tells me you wish to meet with me. I must graciously decline. I do love you and your sister very much, but for my own sake, I must be away from the palace for a season. There is much unrest in my heart, and I need time to heal my exhaustion and pain.

I left after the trial without a goodbye. I am sorry for that, but I knew that words would not change the pain that you would both have to live in for the next few weeks or months. I know it has not been easy.

I feel certain that I know why you want to meet with me. You want to send Eisley away. I have seen from the beginning that you two are as different as night and day. I know that you love each other deeply, but is that enough to rule a kingdom together? I understand your thoughts, and I even see the logic in it, but if you are looking for someone to tell you that this is the right decision, I am not the one.

Katy, you are the Queen. You are grown now. You have been left to stand on your own. You now have to choose if you will stand utterly alone and be the final authority, or if you will rule beside a loved one and share power. Both are difficult. Both come with their share of trials. Who am I to say which is right for you, which is right for Eisley? You must be the one to make this decision.

I suspect you will see me again before the end, Katy, but for now I must go my way and you must go yours. I trust you will do the right thing.

Respectfully Yours,
Billingswaith (Waith)

Katy put the scroll into the roaring fire and leaned her head on the mantle as she watched it burn. She was alone now. Really alone. There was no one left she could go to for wisdom and advice, or even comfort. Her mother, Degrit, Waith....all gone. Eisley was her sister, and she loved her dearly, but she was useless with helping to rule a kingdom.

As the scroll submitted to the flames, she made a decision. She might regret this decision, but a Queen has to be willing to make difficult choices, and she was the Queen.

CHAPTER 35

THE next morning after breakfast, Katy decided it was time to approach Eisley with her plans. Katy sent all the servants out of the room. Eisley sat stroking Cheshire in her lap.

"What is it, Katylove?" she asked.

Katy stood and paced. "Eisley, I think....I think it might be better if we ruled with a little more distance," she said.

Eisley's eyes grew wide. "What do you mean?"

"Well, I just think it would be better if...if there was only one Queen. At least in this region. That way the subjects don't have to split their loyalties." She watched Eisley's face and carried on with caution. "I do most of the royal duties here, and I thought perhaps it would be good if I stayed and you could go to rule over North Wonderland."

Eisley was hurt and surprised, but she nodded and let Katy continue.

"We could have a palace built for you in North Wonderland. You could continue doing what you do best, serving subjects and helping the community."

"I see. So you want to send me away." She stood and set Cheshire on the table, then muttered to herself. "He told me this would happen.

I didn't believe it." She shifted her gaze back to Katy. "I didn't believe it. I thought you would never send me away."

"Who told you this would happen?"

"Degrit. He came last week and gave me a tiara with white roses made of glass. It's beautiful. He told me that you would be sending me away soon. I told him he was crazy, which he is, quite mad, but he was right. How can you do this?" Tears were streaming down Eisley's face now, and Katy couldn't tell if she was angry or hurt or both.

Katy felt a stab of pain. Degrit had given Eisley a crown. He had warned her of Katy's betrayal. Katy's tears had left long ago. That day at Degrit's cottage she had cried her last tear. She had vowed that she would never cry again. She still felt pain though and this hurt went deep.

"I love you, Eisley, and I would never want to hurt you or lose you. But we must think about the kingdom." Katy looked at her with compassion.

Eisley was never one to stay angry, and even now she fell victim to her kind heart. Katy was banishing her to a part of the kingdom that might mean she would never have a firm grip on reality again, but she believed the good intentions Katy spoke of.

"You really think this would be best?" Eisley asked.

Katy sighed and put her hand on Eisley's arm. "I do," she said.

Eisley embraced her. "Oh, I will miss you so much! How will I ever get along without you?" Eisley gushed. Katy smiled and hugged her back.

CHAPTER 36

KATY counted the weeks till Eisley's departure. She wanted to move past living in fear of running into painful memories around every corner. The plans for the North Palace had been drawn up before Katy had even approached Eisley. The workers had already been hired. Moments after the conversation with Eisley, Katy had sent a messenger to tell them that the project was approved and they were to begin construction.

Katy didn't want her sister to be unhappy. She wanted her to have a beautiful place to live. She had even hired Degrit to create gardens around the palace and carve the doors and add any other artistic touches he saw fit. She hadn't spoken with him directly. She had sent messages. He had readily agreed and was currently staying near the building site so that he could work on it while it was being constructed. Katy was amazed that he still managed to work in his wild state of mind, but that was one area that seemed unaffected by his insanity. She was grateful that he was kept busy, because it meant he was less likely to visit Eisley at the palace.

Eisley had become almost excited about her new post. Katy had convinced her that this was best for the kingdom and that all of Wonderland would benefit from this arrangement. It wasn't hard to convince others, — Katy herself believed it. This would be the beginning of a new era for Wonderland.

* * *

It took months for the palace to be finished. There was a large crew of creatures working on it almost nonstop until it was complete. It took longer than expected, because Degrit kept coming up with more ideas and more "finishing touches."

When at last it was finished, word was sent to Katy. She and Eisley spent the day packing up all of Eisley's personal belongings. Katy gathered all the white roses littering the castle and put them in a carriage to go to the North Palace. When Eisley was out of earshot, she told the castle servants she didn't want to see another white rose in the castle for any reason ever. She loved her sister, but it was too painful. It reminded her of lost love and of her own failures.

Katy and Eisley laughed over memories as they rode in the carriage toward the North Palace. The carriage was made for Eisley. It was designed to resemble a white rose and was pulled by a white unicorn. Katy's carriage followed with all of Eisley's belongings. It looked like a blood red rose with black trim around it, and her horse Fleetfoot pulled it. Degrit had designed them both. The contrast was almost as bold as the real life contrast between Katy and Eisley.

When they arrived at the new castle, there was a ceremony and celebration for Eisley's coronation as Queen of North Wonderland. But for all who lived in any part of Wonderland, she would always be the White Queen. She wore the tiara that Degrit had made for her, and it was breathtaking.

The castle was also a work of art. This castle was much smaller and was built of white stone that had been intricately carved. There were vines with white roses carved into the walls and angels at the tops of the turrets. It was perfect for Eisley.

Katy knew this was the ideal palace for her sister. The artist hadn't been exaggerating her beauty or goodness with his work. Looking on it felt toxic to Katy. She could never be what Eisley was so naturally, even if she tried with everything she had. Eisley's light blinded Katy and made her lose sight of any goodness she might possess.

After the coronation, the celebration began. Degrit rose and walked to the podium. Katy hadn't even noticed that he was there. He wore a top hat and bow tie for the occasion.

"We are so very grateful to be able to give the White Queen this beautiful palace that was created just for her. And the creatures of North Wonderland are so very, very happy to have their own Queen. Long live the White Queen." The crowd shouted the words after him. He giggled as he stepped back to let the rest of the proceedings happen.

When the speeches had all been given, the dancing began. The party was in full swing. Katy found Degrit sipping tea at a small table in the courtyard. Nash sat beside him, twitching and occasionally sipping tea.

They looked lost in thought — or perhaps lack of thought. Katy cleared her throat, and both were startled back into the present. Degrit stood and bowed low. Nash hid himself under the table.

"Your Majesty, how very nice to see you. I feel we have met before, yes? You remind me of someone from a dream." He gazed off into the distance, trying to locate a memory that could no longer be found. "Have you met the March Hare?" Degrit asked, excitedly changing the subject. A paw stuck out from beneath the table and Katy shook it.

"You did a very fine job on the palace," Katy said. Degrit seemed very confused when he looked into her eyes.

"Why is a raven like a writing desk?" he whispered.

"I'm sure I don't know," Katy answered. She curtsied politely and left the table. She cursed her heart for clinging to false hope. The tangle of memories that they shared would never again be at the front of his mind. She told hope to leave her alone. All it ever brought was pain.

Katy stayed until Eisley was settled in her new room and they had shared dinner together. They embraced each other as Katy headed toward her carriage. It looked almost frightening in the darkness.

"We will see each other often, won't we?" Eisley asked.

"Of course," Katy lied. She knew that Eisley would soon forget that promise along with many other things, but she also knew that Eisley would be happy here. She felt pleased with the outcome of the move.

She went to her carriage to gather one last gift for Eisley. She handed her a wriggling ball of fur.

"You take Ches. He loves you best anyway," Katy said.

Eisley hugged her again. "Thank you, thank you. I am so grateful that you are my sister," she said. She waved as Katy rode away. Katy felt the darkness of the carriage and the night filling her heart. She had once stood up for the weak; now she manipulated them into doing her will.

CHAPTER 37

IT had been nearly a year since Eisley had moved out. Katy had visited her once, at her request. She was happy and busy with the work of being Queen. North Wonderland had had its effect on her, but not as Katy expected. She wasn't insane or loopy. She just seemed to possess that same childlike happiness. She had lost her concern for most things that didn't matter and seemed more at peace than ever.

Katy was very efficient and hardworking, but her subjects resented her. Since she had sent Eisley away, there had been a massive migration to North Wonderland. It seemed the public would rather risk going insane than live under her rule.

Lutwidge was still loyal to her, and she was grateful for his presence and his counsel. He was still head of the guards, but he also helped Katy with difficult decisions. He had taken over Waith's position in a way. It helped Katy not feel so alone.

Lutwidge met with Katy every week. This week had been particularly difficult because they had just received word that Degrit (now known by the nickname "The Mad Hatter") had moved to North Wonderland. Lutwidge feared they would lose even more of their subjects because of this. The people loved their artist.

"Your M-Majesty, I do have a suggestion. I think it's important to change public opinion of you, to m-make you more approachable, m-more human." Lutwidge began. Katy nodded and he continued. "You are of age for m-marriage now, and I think m-maybe it w-would be helpful if the kingdom saw you in a r-relationship." Katy leaned back in her chair and sighed heavily. "I realize this is a lot to think about. I j-just wanted you to c-consider it. Please," he finished.

"I'll think about it, Lutwidge," she said. When he was gone and she was alone, she let herself turn it over in her mind. She had never pictured herself spending her life alone, but since Degrit, she just wasn't certain. She knew she couldn't let anyone into the inner workings of her heart again. It was dangerous and unpredictable territory. She was controlled and without emotion on the outside, but inside, a dark storm threatened to consume her on an almost daily basis.

She couldn't let anyone in, but perhaps that didn't rule out marriage. She could still get married. It would produce the same results in the kingdom. Her subjects didn't need to know that marriage was only for her image. She could find a man who looked good and knew how to act the part.

* * *

The next day, Katy found Lutwidge in his office. He sat scrawling on a large pile of paperwork. His desk had a picture of him with his new wife. They were smiling and laughing together. Katy tried not to look at it as she started speaking.

"Lutwidge, I've been thinking about our conversation." Lutwidge stood abruptly and bowed when he heard her voice. She continued, "Please sit. I just wanted to tell you, I think you're right," she said. She cleared her throat. "I think we should begin the search to find a suitable match."

Lutwidge nodded. His face was very serious. Katy thought it was funny how something that was greeted with such joy and excitement by so many could feel so close to a death.

"Your Majesty, I have a young m-man I would like to recommend. He lives in a v-village that is nearly four hours from here on horseback. He is very honorable. He has b-been most helpful to me in searching out information about the b-bear involved in the Queen's death. His name is Rean. He lives with h-his brother, Marek, who is very simple. Rean takes care of him. I think he c-could be quite suitable f-for you," Lutwidge watched for Katy's reaction.

"Send a message to him. Have him come to the palace so that we can meet," she said. Lutwidge bowed and began drafting the message.

Katy walked into the hallway and took a deep breath. She touched her temple with a shaking hand. Then she steadied herself and headed to her room, the one place in the palace where she allowed herself to feel.

CHAPTER 38

REAN arrived at the castle on the appointed day. It was cold and snowy. Katy sat in her room drinking tea and watching for him from her window. She hadn't eaten for the last two days. Her nerves were right on top of her skin.

The flakes falling from the sky were silent as they danced in front of her window before continuing their descent. It brought her some calm to watch them. She leaned forward when she heard horses coming into the courtyard.

Rean dismounted from a grey mare. He was tall and muscular. His hair was nearly the same color as Degrit's. Katy took a long deep breath and braced herself.

As she came down the hallway toward the dining room where Rean waited for her, she could hear his voice. It was deep and rich. She wanted to dislike him. That would be easiest. Then it would be an act and nothing more. No emotion would be involved.

She turned the corner and came into the room. Lutwidge and Rean both stood and bowed as she entered. Lutwidge introduced them and Katy had her first close up look at Rean.

His hair, while the same color as Degrit's, was short and tamed. Degrit's eyes were wild and green like the forest. Rean's eyes were dark and brown, but there was warmth to them. He was strong and stood like a soldier.

They sat and had a formal dinner with Lutwidge. It was awkward and felt longer than it should have. Afterwards, Lutwidge suggested they take a walk and get to know each other.

Rean draped Katy's coat around her shoulders as they walked out into the courtyard.

"Wow, I thought that meal would never end. I'm so glad we can speak freely now," he said. He was smiling and Katy noticed how his mouth shifted to one side as he did so. He was very likable with his warm brown eyes and sideways smile. Katy fortified her heart and reminded herself that this was a business deal.

"Yes, it's nice to be out in the fresh air," she said. "So, tell me about yourself, Rean."

He laughed.

"Well, there is not much to tell, I'm afraid. My father is a builder and my mother is a teacher. I am the oldest of two. My brother, Marek, was born before his time. His mind is not what it should be." He looked at his feet as they crunched through the snow. "My mother always wanted a large family, but after Marek...well, he kept them very busy." He smiled at Katy. "My parents are old now and are unable to care for Marek, so he lives with me. I love him very much, but he is quite a handful." He chuckled to himself. "I am in leadership in my village. I am second to the mayor. I like what I do, but I love to get out and work with my hands. So I sometimes help with local building projects." He cleared his throat. "I haven't spent much time around women — I've been too busy with Marek and work. So please forgive me if I seem like an amateur. It's only because I am one." They laughed together. "What about you? I would love to hear more about you."

Katy hesitated. *I am a heartless Queen who hurts everyone she comes in contact with,* she thought.

"Well, I'm sure you've heard a lot of it already. I came from the Shadowlands when I was young. I don't remember much from that world anymore. I was taught all about life here in Wonderland by — " She hesitated. She didn't want to speak about Waith or Degrit. That part of her history was hers alone; she didn't want to give it away. " — by some very good tutors. I had several very wonderful and happy years here before my mother was killed. Then Eisley and I became Queens, and now she, too, is gone." She could hear the ice in her voice.

Rean looked at her intently. "I am so sorry about your mother. I know the last few years must have been very hard." She avoided his eyes as she smiled a thank you. "It must have been hard when you first arrived here, too, losing your family and starting over," he said.

"Actually, it was like a dream that had come true. I had a very sad existence in the Shadowlands. My parents were very inconvenienced by my presence, and I didn't have friends to speak of. When I arrived here, I found a family that had been waiting for me and loved me before they even met me. It was like a story from one of my books had come true." They sat together on a bench near a large outdoor fireplace in the courtyard. "It was like a fairy tale. It had some scary moments, too, as any good story."

"Like the billdralls?" he asked. She looked at him in surprise. "Sorry...I...well, I've done my research on you." He smiled his sideways grin again.

"No, it's fine. Um...yes...the billdralls was definitely a scarier moment in my past. I was stupid and tried to sneak out at night on my own. I nearly ended my story there," she said.

"Why were you sneaking out?" he asked. She could see genuine curiosity on his face. She put her hand on his knee.

"Listen, here's the truth. I need to get married. My subjects hate me. They think I'm the reason that Eisley nearly died, and now that she's gone, well, they blame me." Her words came quickly, a confession she couldn't get out fast enough. "You seem like a very kind man, but I just want you to know that I am not offering my heart to you or anyone else. I just need a man to stand in and be there. Maybe someone that could turn the hearts of my subjects. I see that you could do that. I just want you to know what you are getting into. Think of this as more of an arranged marriage than a marriage for love."

He looked into her eyes and reached for her hair. He rubbed the black strands between his fingers and then tucked them behind her ear.

"You know, I saw you for the first time at the coronation. I couldn't take my eyes off of you. I'd never seen such beauty. And your hair, it was amazing. As black as night." Katy stared at her lap as he continued, "I can see that something's happened since that day. I won't ask what it was. I can see in your eyes. Something's gone." He put his hand on top of hers. "I fell in love that day. I want you to have the chance to love me, too. I'll say yes to your proposition, but on two conditions."

Katy held her breath.

"The first is that my brother be allowed to come here and live in the palace, too." Katy nodded and smiled at the suggestion. "The second is that you let me love you, and who knows? Maybe someday you'll love me too." He smiled and she kissed his cheek.

"I can agree to those," she said. Then her face turned serious. "But don't get your hopes up. I'm a lost cause." He smiled and his charm was effortless.

"I don't believe in lost causes." He leaned forward to kiss her. She stood abruptly and headed toward the castle. He followed after her.

"I'll contact Ms. Pinkington. She can arrange all the wedding details. I would prefer a small wedding, if that's all right with you." She turned to him. He was chuckling to himself.

"Whatever you want, my dear," he said. She wasn't sure what she wanted and she didn't like the way she felt around him. He was already causing unrest in her well-guarded heart.

CHAPTER 39

KATY tried very hard to steer clear of all the wedding preparations. She busied herself with her royal duties. Ms. Pinkington was thrilled to have been given all the responsibility. The kingdom was soon buzzing with the news of a new member of the royal family. Some were hopeful that Katy might be changing and becoming more like her sister.

Ms. Pinkington had suggested that perhaps it would be charming to have a herald at the wedding to blow a trumpet and announce things. Katy agreed, as long as the wedding stayed small. The herald was later brought to Katy for her approval.

He was a small white rabbit with a waistcoat and a pocket watch. His fidgeting mannerisms reminded her of another rabbit she knew. He bowed and cleared his throat.

"Your Majesty, I am William Herald Rabbit of the Warren family. I have played the trumpet since my youth, and I am a most excellent reader."

"The Warren family?" Katy asked. "Are you Nash's brother?" The rabbit looked shocked and slightly embarrassed.

"Yes, ma'am, I am afraid that I am indeed the sibling of that poor

171

insane chap, but I assure you I will be very responsible and unlike my brother in every way," he said.

"It's all right, William. I'm quite fond of your brother. I knew him before he was mad," she said.

"Yes, Your Majesty, I remember your visit to our home very well. It was before...everything."

Katy smiled. She understood perfectly what the little rabbit meant.

"Indeed it was," she answered. "Ms. Pinkington, I think that little William here will be exactly the herald that we need in our palace. Thank you for finding him."

"Thank you, Your Majesty," William said, and bowed again before exiting the room. Katy smiled at the little white rabbit. He was so like Nash...before. She let her mind wander for a moment to "before" and wished she hadn't. The pain was still too great.

* * *

Over the next several months leading up to the wedding, Rean and Katy had many meetings together, but Katy made certain that they were rarely alone.

When their wedding day arrived, it was small and elegant. It was held in a little chapel near the palace. The chapel had all but erupted in red roses and sterlings. It was beautiful.

Lutwidge walked Katy down the aisle. She looked at the front toward Rean. He was beautiful. His brother, Marek, was swaying next to him, a sloppy grin on his face. Katy had met him a couple times, and his brutal honesty made her increasingly uncomfortable. Eisley stood at the front, smiling widely as Katy walked forward.

The wedding was a much more subdued event than Eisley's and, thankfully, contained much less drama. The reception afterward was held in the courtyard. Everything was decorated perfectly. The bride and groom sat at a table in the center where all the guests could come and greet them.

Katy smiled and played her part. She looked through the crowd, wondering where Lutwidge had gone. Suddenly, she spotted a painfully familiar face. Degrit was at a table alone. He lifted a glass to her as she spotted him. His eyes looked clear at the moment, and she caught her breath.

Rean leaned toward her. "Are you all right?" He followed her line of sight to Degrit's table. She looked away and shook her head.

"Yes, fine, sorry. Um...can you excuse me for a moment?" She stood before he answered. She walked straight to Degrit's table and sat across from him. His eyes were swimming in pain.

"Hello, Raven. You look stunning," he whispered. Katy felt tears threatening to fill her eyes. She fought them.

"Degrit, you're here, and you remember?" He grabbed her hand under the table.

"Katylove, I'm so sorry. What I have done, it's unforgivable. I removed the danglias the day after you came to see me, but the damage had already been done, I'm afraid." His thumb rubbed her hand as he spoke.

"But you seem so sane," Katy whispered.

Degrit sighed. "I have moments. They never last long and usually serve only to push me into a deep depression about the reality I've forced on myself. But when I woke this morning, my mind was clear, and I had to come see you one more time. I'd forgotten it was your wedding day." His eyes began to fill with tears. "I just want to tell you to be happy. He seems a very likable chap. I'm not really sure about his

173

brother, though. I think he might be a bit mad," he joked. "Be happy, Katylove. Take this second chance. Please."

"Degrit, this should have been us," she whispered.

"No, Katylove, you mustn't think like that. I'm not worth much these days. I'm a raving lunatic most of the time. You deserve something better, and I'm happy to see that you got it." He wiped his eyes. As he stood to walk away, Katy followed him. She looked back to see the wedding guests were distracted with dancing and drinks. Rean was smiling and shaking hands with a smartly dressed marmoset. He glanced at her from the corner of his eye as she disappeared into the forest.

Degrit was sitting on their bench. She sat beside him and let her head rest on his shoulder. He put his hand on her cheek.

"Raven, I'm sorry for what we lost." He used his other hand to wipe his tears that seemed to fall with no sign of stopping. "I'm sorry for coming today, but it's so rare that I'm this lucid, and I wanted to tell you that I know what I did was wrong and I am so sorry."

Katy felt her heart being shredded. She looked at him.

"I'm different now, Degrit. You wouldn't want me anyway," she said.

He picked up her chin and looked into her eyes. "You're the same girl I have always been in love with. You've had to learn how to be strong in a way you never should have had to." He kissed her lips gently, then stood to leave. "I'm sorry, Katylove. I must go now. Please be happy. Please take your second chance. Live your life." He stood and walked away into the woods, and Katy let herself drop to the bench. She touched her cheek where Degrit's hand had been. It was warm, but dry. She didn't even remember how to cry.

"Are you alright, love?" The voice startled her back to reality. She looked up to see Rean. His brows were furrowed with concern. Katy put her head in her hands and sighed. She felt Rean sit next to her. He sat in silence and rubbed her back as she tried to wrestle the demons in her heart back into submission.

"Rean, I'm sorry," she spoke with her head down.

"No need. I think you gave me fair warning the day I met you." He was smiling, but there was sadness behind it.

"Thank you for being so gracious. Shall we go and keep up appearances?" she suggested. He stood and held out his hand for her. She kissed his cheek. She knew that Degrit was right. This was a second chance, but something in her refused to allow her to find happiness a second time.

CHAPTER 40

AFTER the wedding celebrations were over, Rean and Katy climbed into the carriage that Degrit had designed and headed to their honeymoon. Katy didn't know where they were going. She didn't really care. She was glad to be away from the palace for a few days, even if it meant she had to be alone with Rean.

When they arrived, the sunlight was fading, but she could see the cottage. It was beautiful. It looked like it had been constructed by the same architects who had built the palace.

"Lutwidge told me about this place. He said you've never been here. It was built the same time as the palace. It was designed as a place for the royal family to have some time to themselves. But apparently it was one of the king's favorite places, and after his death the family couldn't bear to come here any longer," he explained.

Katy sighed. "It's perfect," she said.

"And that," he said, pointing, "is the Babbling Brook. Have you ever seen it?" he asked.

"A long time ago."

"Did it speak to you?"

A tender heart...a raven with feathers of satin...speaking words that bring comfort. Strong in love...vulnerable in pain. Guard your heart. Hold to who you know yourself to be right now.

She remembered the words like it was yesterday, but could hardly remember the girl she was then.

"Yes, but it was just nonsense," she lied.

* * *

Night came quickly. The little cottage was illuminated with crystals that seemed to float about the room. Rean had arranged a beautiful dinner. They sat at the table and Katy tried her best to pretend to eat.

Rean rambled about the day and the creatures he had met. Katy was a ghost. She thanked him for the meal and walked out to the brook. She may have interrupted him in the middle of something he was saying, but she couldn't be sure.

The air was cold and humid. She pulled her shoes off and dipped her feet into the icy stream. She imagined herself under the water. Staying down until all the fight was gone and floating away with no more pain. Fiddle trees were playing in the wind some distance away, and Katy waited. Rean watched her in secret from the doorway. The whispers came first, and she sat up straighter when she heard them. The haunting voice followed.

"Let his hands hold your heart. He can protect it. Let go of what you once held to. You are not the one you once were."

Katy jumped up and threw her shoes into the black waters.

"You useless body of water! I hate you!! You don't understand anything about me!!" she yelled. She felt something touch her and realized that Rean was behind her wrapping a blanket around her. She was so startled that it took a moment to catch her breath. When she did, she noticed for the first time that night that she was cold to the bone. Her skin was purple and she was shivering uncontrollably. How long had she been sitting by the brook? She turned to face Rean.

He gathered her up in his arms and held her while she sobbed. Dry cries with no tears. Rean picked her up and carried her into the cottage. He had a steaming bath prepared for her. He helped her get undressed and slip into the hot water. The shivering finally subsided, and the crying noises eventually faded into the water.

When she stepped out of the bath, Rean wrapped her in a towel and carried her to bed. She curled into the fetal position. Rean sat beside her on the bed. He stroked her hair.

"I hope someday you'll let me into your heart," he whispered. Katy fell into a deep dreamless sleep.

CHAPTER 41

KATY awoke to an empty cottage with sunlight streaming in the windows. The table beside the bed had a plate of cut fruit and a steaming cup of tea. As she stood, her towel slipped off. She tried to cover herself with her hands as she remembered the night before. She quickly located her clothes and slipped into a simple blue dress. She was embarrassed thinking of Rean helping her into the bath.

"Good morning." Rean spoke in soft, deep tones. Katy was desperately attempting to tame her wild hair into a braid.

"Morning." Her hair finally submitted, and Katy reached for the tea beside the bed. Rean was dressed in a white cotton shirt and brown pants that had been rolled up to his knees. He filled the kettle and put it over the fire to boil.

"How are you feeling?" He stared intently at her. Katy looked away. He looked right through her, into her soul. She felt like she'd forgotten to get dressed.

"Better, thanks," she said. They sat at the table across from each other. "I'm sorry about everything yesterday."

"No need to apologize. I don't suppose I can get any explanation?"

He put his hand on hers to reassure her. Katy sighed. She knew he deserved one.

"Well..." she took another deep breath. "I was in love once. It was beautiful. But I destroyed it. It's what I do. I find good things and tear them apart." She looked into her tea cup as she spoke.

"So that's it. The coronation. Degrit, you were in love with him?" Rean spoke tenderly.

She winced as he said Degrit's name. "Yes. We loved each other. But once it was known that he was an artist, our love was forbidden."

He rubbed her hand. "I met him once. Forgive me, but he didn't seem to be completely sane."

"Well, he started growing danglias in his cottage just after everything happened. By the time I found out, it was too late. He was quite sane before he met me."

"He was at the wedding." He pulled the boiling kettle from the fire, refilled Katy's cup, then poured his own.

"Yes. But he was...he was as he used to be. He said he has moments of sanity and he wanted to apologize while he was in his right mind."

"Yes, I've heard that with other victims of danglia toxin. They have brief moments of clarity. I'm so sorry, Katy. That must have been difficult for you."

She looked into his eyes and could see that he was genuine. "He told me this was my second chance. That I had to take it. To be happy."

"It sounds like he really loves you," he said. She smiled absently. He went to the kitchen and began putting jam and butter on a piece of bread.

"Rean? Did you hear what the brook said to me last night?"

His eyes were filled with compassion when he looked at her. "I did. And after hearing a little of your story, I know you aren't ready for me to hold your heart. You're hardly ready for me to hold your *hand*. But I'll do all I can to take care of you and love you well, Katy." Katy couldn't look at him. He was too good for her. She wanted him to run from her. She wanted to warn him that her heart had begun to turn as black as her hair, but he wouldn't believe her if she told him.

"Were you at the brook?" She glanced down at his rolled up pants and bare feet.

"Yes," he smirked.

"Did she speak?" Katy asked. He sighed and looked down at the table.

"She did. She said that I would find happiness in the shadows. She said that I was loyal and true, that I should have the courage to stand up for myself." His eyes met Katy's. "It's all a bit cryptic, isn't it? Just sane enough to make you think it means something, but crazy enough to make you wonder what in the universe it could be talking about."

They laughed together and felt some of the tension leave the room.

* * *

Katy and Rean had four days at the cabin before they returned to reality. Katy enjoyed a fantasy where her life was her own. There were no subjects, no crown, no public opinion, and no insane artist she had once loved. She gave herself to Rean. She *loaned* herself to him, knowing she would jerk it all away when they returned to the palace. This was the land of pretend, and she welcomed the chance to be a blushing bride to a kind and handsome man who adored her.

Rean felt that he was really beginning to break through. She seemed to be giving her heart to him. She trusted him and even let him love her the way he wanted. He didn't know yet what real life would hold, and he didn't have time to prepare his heart. It was easier when he knew she didn't love him. Now, his heart was in a very vulnerable place as he felt her returning his feelings and giving herself to him.

CHAPTER 42

THE last day at the cottage seemed to slip through their fingers. The sun was setting, and the colors of the sky were turning orange and purple just as it felt the day had started. Katy hated to leave. She stood in the kitchen of her pretend life. She could have done this. She would have been a good wife. She could have led a normal life and been happy. Rean came behind her and wrapped his arms around her.

"It's hard to leave, isn't it?" he whispered. All she could manage was a weak nod.

They packed up and boarded the carriage that waited for them. Katy watched out the window as the trees gave way to houses and then again to trees and then a courtyard that was all too familiar.

Rean stepped out and helped Katy down the steps. The palace staff was lining the doorway to welcome them home. Katy and Rean were congratulated and given flowers and trinkets.

When they got upstairs, Katy started toward her room, when Rean caught her arm.

"This way, love," he reminded her. Katy had left her old room exactly as it was. She told the staff that no one was to use it except her.

It was her sanctuary. She needed it. She didn't tell Rean about it. He didn't need to know. He wouldn't understand why she had to have a place to be away from him.

When they opened the door to their room, they found Marek sitting on the edge of their large bed bouncing up and down.

"Knave of Hearts, I'm the knave. That's what they call me, 'cuz that's what I am. I am a knave, Rean. Rean, I'm the Knave of Hearts. That's what they told me. That's what I am." He was grinning and blinking obsessively as he spoke.

Rean embraced his brother. "Yes, I know. It's good to see you, Marek."

"I was sad because I missed you because you weren't here and I missed you. You were gone a long time." His face turned sad as though he might start crying. Katy was just wishing she had somewhere else to be so that she wouldn't have to speak to him.

Rean held him by the shoulders and spoke sternly. "Marek, we are home now. You don't need to miss me anymore. No more sad thoughts."

Marek blinked thoughtfully for several moments before giving in to a big dopey grin. His gaze shifted to Katy.

"She pretends. She's a liar 'cuz she doesn't tell the truth and she pretends." He pointed and advanced as he spoke. Rean grabbed his arm.

"Marek, that's Katy. She's my wife. I don't want you to speak like that again. Do you understand?" Rean sounded very near anger. Marek was nodding with widened eyes. Rean escorted him into the hallway and down the hall to his room. When he returned, Katy was sitting on the bed in silence.

"I'm sorry about that. He just says whatever crazy thing he thinks.

Please don't let it upset you." Rean sat beside her on the bed. He touched her arm.

He's not crazy, she thought. *He's the only one who sees me for what I truly am.* She was back now. Back to real life. Life with control and without emotion, life behind the wall. She smiled at Rean and kissed his cheek.

CHAPTER 43

KATY woke suddenly and sat bolt upright in bed. Rean was standing at the window. There was a terrifying roar outside. It sounded like something devouring the entire kingdom.

"What is it?" Katy asked. She came to the window and stood near Rean.

"It's a shadow storm. The last one came when I was only a small boy. Dark clouds swirling overhead and a terrifying roar, but the worst part of a shadow storm is that when it's over, so many are gone." He put his arm around her. They'd been home now for several weeks, and Katy had kept herself so busy that they hardly had a moment alone, which is exactly how she wanted it.

"What do you mean?" she whispered.

"Wherever the storm hits, creatures will be missing. It takes them. No one knows where. They just vanish. I lost my best friend when I was a boy. Her name was Eelna. She was wild and free and full of life. The morning after the storm, I ran to her house as I did every morning, and I found her mother crying on the front steps. Her father told me she left with the storm."

Katy shuddered. A part of her hoped she would be caught up in it and taken somewhere else. Another life, another start. Rean held her hand through the howling night, and when first light came, they went down to start the work of helping their kingdom rebuild.

* * *

Katy knew that compassion was not her strong suit. She sent Rean out into the villages for a several-day tour to find out what they needed and how the Queen could help them. She stayed at the palace, caring for the creatures that came in seeking help.

When Rean returned, he was dirty and tired. His eyes were puffy and red. He looked as though he had spent most of his return trip sobbing. He dismounted and walked to Katy and kissed her hard. She tried not to show her discomfort with this gesture.

"Are you all right?" she asked. "What's the state of things?"

He rubbed his face with his hands. "Structurally there is very little damage. The homes and buildings are almost all intact. There are some trees down, but not many. But there are many creatures missing. Many children have become orphans. I made a decision to build a children's home in Lewisville. I think we could dispatch some of the guards to help with clean-up and make a request for volunteers to help with the building of the center and that would....that would be all we could do to help for now."

Katy could see tears threatening to fall as he spoke. She hugged him. "I'm sorry. That must have been so hard for you. Thank you."

"I'm going to bathe and sleep, and then I am heading out to make this center happen. I'm going to take Marek with me. He's actually quite good with his hands. So he won't be around to harass you. But

I'm not sure how long I'll be gone."

Katy put her hands on his face. "Take as much time as you need."
He kissed her hands and headed up to his room to get some much
needed rest.

CHAPTER 44

REAN was gone for four months. He came back to see Katy as often as he could, but he was in charge of the project so he couldn't neglect it long. Katy was glad for the break and was relieved to have Marek elsewhere for a while.

When the center was finished, Katy came to the celebration and congratulated Rean on an amazing job. He took her aside during all the festivities. He stopped at a back room that looked like a sewing room of sorts and sat her down in one of the small chairs.

"Katy, I have something I want to ask you about. It's an idea, and you might think it's crazy, but I hope not." Rean was nervous, and Katy could see that whatever he was about to suggest meant a lot to him. "There are several children here I have grown very fond of. They have become very, very dear to me. The palace is so large. We have so much space. I just...I was just thinking that maybe we could use a wing of the palace for these kids. We could, you know, sort of adopt them. We could hire more staff to help teach them and take care of them. I just...I know it's crazy, but I think it would just be so great to have children in the palace, and you'll love them." He stopped and looked anxiously into her eyes. "And they'll love you."

"Rean, I'm not very good with children."

"It's all right. You'll learn. Besides, the staff and I will do the work. You can just enjoy them," he said.

Katy thought about it. They did have plenty of room and staff to care for them. And it would keep Rean occupied. She could lead her own life while he was busy with the children. He was the closest to her. If she could manage to keep distance from him, her control would be much easier to maintain and her emotions were much less likely to rear their ugly heads.

"I think...I think it's a grand idea," she stated.

Rean clapped his hands together and kissed her cheek. "I want you to meet them." He went into the hallway and called for the kids who must have been in the next room.

They filed into the tiny room, and Katy thought they would never stop coming.

"How many of them are there?" she asked.

"Ten," he said. He introduced each of them. They looked like a set of Russian dolls Katy had seen long ago in the Shadowlands, going from tallest to smallest all lined up in order. There were six girls and four boys. The oldest was a boy with dark eyes and auburn hair, and two in the middle were boys, ginger and fidgety. They were all beautiful. One of the little girls reminded Katy of Rean's description of Eelna. She was the smallest. Her hair was a long, wild, blond mess and her eyes were full of mischief. Hers was the only name Katy remembered that day — Leyla, a wild little girl full of fire. She smiled at all of them and shook their hands politely. She knew that theirs would never be a mother/child relationship, but Rean was anxious to be their caregiver. She would let him play his part and she would be free to play hers.

* * *

When they returned home with ten children, the palace staff was overjoyed. They went out of their way to do whatever they could to make sure the children were happy and comfortable. Katy noticed that people looked at her differently now. She was a mother. Rean's idea had been an even better one than she'd realized.

CHAPTER 45

WHEN Eisley got word of the adoption, she sent a message asking the entire family to come visit her at her palace. She and Rean had hit it off the moment they met. Katy knew they would. They were kindred spirits.

They had made the arrangements and were now heading out to spend the weekend with Eisley in North Wonderland. Katy and Rean traveled in Katy's carriage. The kids followed in a larger carriage with two nannies.

When they arrived, Eisley was standing in the courtyard anxiously. She clapped her hands with joy as the carriages came into view.

The children were surprised when Eisley lifted each one of them into a tight embrace. Katy had barely touched them. Katy could see Auntie Eisley would be a new favorite, and she guessed some of them would even be wishing for her as their mother by the end of the weekend.

Eisley ushered everyone inside for a feast. There was a huge table set up in the dining area. All of them fit around it. The kids were buzzing with excitement. Eisley interviewed each child and learned more about them than Katy had cared to ask. She saw them as if for the first time when she saw them through Eisley's eyes.

After lunch they adjourned to the courtyard, where Eisley introduced them to a new sport very popular in North Wonderland. It was very much like croquet, which Katy had vague memories of from the Shadowlands. Instead of mallets, however, you held a flamingo, and instead of a ball, you hit a hedgehog.

Katy had opted to watch. She sat at a table watching Eisley and *her* husband and children laughing and enjoying one another. Cheshire was there, too. He was disappearing and reappearing. The children were delighted with him. He was also old enough to speak now, although he didn't bother speaking to Katy.

"You should get up and play." The voice was small and insistent. Katy looked down to see Leyla in front of her, her hands planted firmly on her hips.

"Pardon?"

"We like you. We want you to come play with us."

Katy was without words for a moment. She sat, jaw open.

Leyla shook her head, then ran back over to the rest of the group. Katy sat in shock for several moments before she realized that Leyla was being sincere. She walked over and joined the group. Leyla smiled at her knowingly.

Once Katy joined the game, she found herself laughing and forgetting about the storm inside her for a moment. She discovered that she was quite good at flamingo croquet. Rean smiled at her and thanked her for joining them.

* * *

The next day Eisley's dear friend, the Duchess, came for a visit. Her face was old and gnarled, but her eyes were smiling and sharp. The children loved her immediately. She took them on a long walk to see North Wonderland. When they returned, the children were bursting at the seams to tell all they had seen.

Rean and Eisley took them into the palace for purple blots and tea. The Duchess invited Katy to sit with her at a table in the courtyard. The staff brought pink lemonade.

As they sat sipping their cold drinks, Katy could feel the Duchess sizing her up.

"Darling, you are in a fix aren't you?" Her voice was gravelly.

"Pardon?"

"You heard me."

"Yes, I did, but I have no idea what you mean," Katy stated. The Duchess laughed loud and long. Katy began to think she was perhaps one of the more insane residents of North Wonderland.

"Well, then, let me explain myself. You, my dear, are a truly gifted actress, and I would bet that most people buy your act without a second thought. But you see, I am not most people." She pulled her white gloves off as she continued. "I am just crazy enough to look beyond what I see. You know that Eisley would have been a much better Queen than you. That's why you sent her away. You are married only to make the kingdom believe you still have a heart, and you care nothing for those children. They give you an excuse to ignore Rean. Did I miss anything?"

"I didn't send Eisley away. You don't know anything. How dare you?" Katy was surprised and hurt.

"How? Well, I think you're really looking for the why, and the why is that I have grown very fond of Eisley. And the more I see of you and how you rule this kingdom, the more I despise you. And I'm not the only one. You can bet on that."

"Oh, really?" Katy felt her caged anger escaping.

"Yes, really. I tell you all this because I am giving you the opportunity to step down. Step down or be thrown down!"

"Why should I step down? I have done nothing wrong, and Eisley *wants* to be here! I rule the kingdom to the best of my ability, and Eisley loves North Wonderland!" Katy wondered how much of her past and her mind was littered with justification. She had sent Eisley away for selfish reasons. Did she really rule her kingdom in a way that was best for her subjects or best for herself?

The Duchess stared into her face for a long, quiet moment. "Child, I am giving you grace, an opportunity to apologize and set things straight. It's not my fault if you are too stupid to take the chance."

"What do you mean?" She knew that she wasn't hugely popular with some of her subjects, but it was painful to hear this open hatred toward her.

"The entire kingdom has watched the way you have treated Eisley, the rightful Queen, tearing her love from her. Killing Thaddeus ruthlessly, then standing by apathetically as she withered away almost to death. Then, at the first opportunity, you send her away to North Wonderland, hoping she will lapse into insanity, no doubt. She is the Queen's true daughter. You were not even born of the Queen. You don't even have the same blood in your veins."

"You would have me step down and have Eisley rule the entire kingdom?" Katy's hands were forming themselves into tight fists.

"Not just me, dear. There are many. We don't want to be ruled by the Bloody Queen!"

"The Bloody Queen?" It was the first time Katy had heard this cruel nickname.

"Yes, dear, the blood on your hands is barely dried, and you are trying to pretend you are a mother and a wife...with capacity for love. Well, darling, we all know that in order to love, one must first have a heart!"

Katy stormed off. She couldn't stand to listen to another word.

"That is it! I've heard enough!!" She summoned the guards and had the Duchess arrested. "I want her taken to my palace and placed in the dungeon." She had more questions that she needed answered. What did the Duchess mean, there were many?

The guards did as they were told. They walked the old lady toward the carriage.

"Just remember, dear, you had your chance. When you see white roses, just remember. I'm not the only one, and one day Eisley will be on your throne as she should have been from the start!" She shouted the words from the window as the carriage started off.

Katy stood watching the carriage drive away. She felt as though she had just taken a hearty swig of poison. Her stomach was a tight knot, and the wall she hid behind, her protection, began to feel like a prison that was slowly suffocating her.

When the rest of the family came out to the courtyard to say their goodbyes, Katy didn't have the heart to tell Eisley what had happened. She told her that the Duchess had rushed off to another appointment.

The children were terribly sad to leave, but they left with promises of another visit soon and a gift of flamingos and hedgehogs for playing their own games back home.

Katy left heavy with regret. Visits with her sister often did that to her.

CHAPTER 46

KATY knew that Rean would find out about the Duchess sooner or later. She decided to get it over with. They were alone in the carriage. It was the perfect opportunity.

"Rean, I have to talk with you about something that happened."

He sat up and leaned in closer.

"Sure," he said.

"Well, when you all went inside and I was alone with the Duchess...well...she threatened me. She alluded to an underground movement of people wanting to overthrow me and bring Eisley to power over all of Wonderland. She called me a liar and threatened to have me overthrown so I had her taken to the dungeon."

Rean's eyes widened in shock. "You did what?? Why would you do that?"

Katy crossed her arms and pursed her lips. "I think I just told you."

"Katy, she is a crazy old lady. When we went on the walk she took us to her house. She has a pig she thinks is her baby. She dresses it and pushes it around in a pram. She's insane! Not to mention the fact that she's also one of Eisley's dearest friends! You can't do this!"

Katy felt anger like a fire just under her skin.

"Rean! You didn't hear what she said to me!! And last time I checked, I was ruling this kingdom, not you!!"

Katy noticed his jaw tighten as he sat back. She knew she had gone too far.

"You're right, Katy. It's your decision."

He wouldn't finish this fight. He would back down, and she would have her way like she always did. Part of her wished he would stand up to her, tell her she was wrong. But he wouldn't.

The rest of the ride was tense and silent. When they arrived at the palace, Rean nearly jumped from the carriage. Katy stepped out and smiled graciously at the staff lining the courtyard. She laughed with them and told them she was anxious to show them the new game they had learned. Rean walked silently to his room. Katy didn't follow him. She slept in her old room that night.

CHAPTER 47

THE next morning, Lutwidge approached Katy with urgent news. He bowed low and welcomed her home.

"Your Majesty, P-Prontil's son is here and wishes to speak with you immediately. He's had a vision," he said. Katy racked her brain. She knew that name was familiar, but she couldn't place it. Her mind was still muddled from the encounter with the Duchess, her heart still wrestling with all she had said.

"Prontil?" she asked.

"Yes, Your Majesty, the aphid that f-foretold of your coming so long ago."

"Yes! Of course, right. Send him in."

An aphid about the size of a large mouse waddled in. He bowed his head and removed a strange blue hat he was wearing.

"Your Majesty, I am so sorry to intrude this way. But I have had a vision. I lived for many years thinking I was not given my father's gift. Yesterday, all that changed. I was tilling my garden and suddenly everything went black and I saw a girl."

"A girl?" Katy asked.

"Yes, a little girl, and somehow I knew she was from the Shadowlands. She had golden hair and went by the name Alice. She was talking with the old caterpillar — you know, the one in North Wonderland that sits on his mushroom smoking his hookah all day." Katy nodded; she had seen him more than once when visiting North Wonderland. "Then I saw her near a bush of white roses. That is all I know for certain, but, Your Majesty, I think she wants your crown. Why else would she have come?"

Katy nodded. "Thank you for bringing this news. If you have any further visions, please come forward right away," she said. He bowed several times and left the room.

Lutwidge stepped forward again. "Your Majesty, do you want to send a team out? To investigate?"

Katy shook her head. "That won't be necessary," she said. She had a good idea of someone who might know more about this girl.

* * *

Katy didn't generally spend time visiting with prisoners, so the guard was quite surprised to see her in the dungeon. He led her to the Duchess's cell, then hurried back to his post.

The Duchess stood and walked toward the bars.

"Well, to what do I owe this privilege? The Queen herself come down to visit the lowly prisoner?" the Duchess teased.

"I have heard rumors about a girl from the Shadowlands. One who has come to steal my crown. What do you know of her?" Katy tried to stick to the facts and control the fire in her belly.

"Oh, do tell! I've heard no such rumors, but she does sound like my kind of girl. I'm sure we'll be fast friends."

"Is this girl involved in your plans?" Katy asked.

"*My* plans? You think the plans to overthrow you are *my* plans? My dear, the white rose society is spreading all over the kingdom. Don't be so silly as to think a crazy old woman like me is in charge! And I speak the truth when I tell you that I do not know her." She laughed as though she thought Katy to be completely ridiculous. Katy's jaw tightened. She turned to walk away.

"When are you letting me out, Queenie?? I have things to do. I have a child at home," the Duchess yelled down the corridor.

Katy turned to the guard. "I want you to release her. Follow her to her home. Watch her closely. If you see her with this girl with golden hair from the Shadowlands, this Alice, arrest her and bring her back here immediately."

Katy closed the door and didn't look back.

CHAPTER 48

THINGS had grown tense between Katy and Rean. Katy was too involved in her inner turmoil to be available to him. He was still angry with her for what he felt was a wrongful imprisonment, but he lacked the courage to stand up to her. Instead, he made her pay with cold stares and distance. Katy knew he was angry. She was torn. A part of her still wanted to be that wife from the cottage, but another part of her began to lose respect for him. Degrit would never have let Katy act like such a tyrant. He loved her enough to stand up to her.

Rean had learned a lot on the coach ride back from Eisley's palace. He was in love with a dream that was never to be. Katy was never going to let him in. She wanted to control him. She wanted him to play his part. He was heartbroken and began to resent her for it.

Marek continued to offend Katy. Rean did his best to find any way he could to keep them away from each other, but when they met it was always ugly. Now Rean could see that everything that Marek spoke was truth, and that made it so much worse. Rean spent most of his time with the children. Being with Katy was too painful.

Katy became obsessed. She had lost so much in her life. She felt that all she had left was the throne, her position, her crown. She would not have it taken away! She thought about it daily and became more than a little paranoid.

* * *

Years passed. The distance between Katy and Rean had become a gaping cavern. He was kind but lacked courage, and she found nothing to respect in him. She was alone. She trusted no one. She became full of bitterness and hate. She invited it in. It was easier than having a tender heart. She had tried that, and the memory of the pain of it still urged her on. The girl she had once been was gone. She clung now to power where once she had held to love.

Eisley remained the same. Rean and the children would go and visit her quite often, but Katy had stopped visiting many years before. Katy had lost the desire to be near her sister.

Her sentencing of crimes became irrational, handing out death sentences for minor offenses. Rean or Lutwidge would try to find ways around her insanity by setting creatures free secretly or having Katy sign papers that pardoned the offender without her realizing what she was signing. She saw treason in every act. She saw betrayal in every eye. The Queen of Hearts had become a tyrant. She had lived up to her nickname, the Bloody Queen.

* * *

The weather became warmer, and each year at the beginning of the hot season the royal family held a celebration and welcomed guests from all around the countryside. The whole of Wonderland looked forward to it, although lately it had become a terrifying prospect to be anywhere near the Queen. The guests were all anxious and excited, hoping desperately that they would not offend her.

Katy had been informed that the duchess had been returned to the prison. She knew that Alice was in Wonderland now. Her paranoia had reached an all time high as she dressed that morning. She was already seething with anticipation of the day she would finally meet Alice.

The family was all dressed for the occasion, all of them in beautiful clothes adorned with hearts. Wearing Katy's symbol on his own tunic just served to remind Rean of his broken heart. He advised Marek to be quiet near the Queen. To keep him occupied, he gave him a velvety pillow and told him that he had a very special job of carrying his crown. Marek was very proud to have such an important job and didn't think to ask why the King wouldn't just wear the crown.

There was to be a royal procession through the courtyard, followed by a game of flamingo croquet, to start off the celebration. The guards lined up and the family fell in behind them. They marched out the front door and into the bright sunlight. Nash's little brother, the white rabbit, ran up to join the procession, wearing his tunic adorned with hearts and carrying his trumpet. He bowed to the Queen and stepped in line. As they rounded the castle, Katy saw something happening ahead.

White roses! There were two bushes of white roses in full bloom! Who had done this? Was this a signal that the big coup was about to take place? A rose bush would not grow overnight. How long had this been going on in her very own garden? She looked closer to see a small blond girl. Her workers were having an earnest conversation with her. She remembered the aphid's vision about the visitor from the

Shadowlands near the white roses and felt certain that this must be the famous Alice.

As they approached the scene, she felt hot anger welling up and escaping with each breath. The cards (as they sometimes referred to the palace staff) fell flat on their faces. The girl stood obstinately without even a curtsy.

"Who is this?" Katy demanded, looking toward Marek. He grinned his sloppy grin and blinked several times.

"Idiot!" she muttered as she turned to Alice. "What's your name, child?" She coated her words with honey hoping to appear sympathetic toward the girl.

"My name is Alice, if you please, Your Majesty," she said.

"And who are they?" Katy asked pointing to the cards lying face down, hoping to undercover the conspiracy.

"How should *I* know? It's no business of mine," the girl snapped.

Katy felt heat in her face and tightened her hands into fists. It would be easiest to just be rid of this pimple of a threat.

"Off with her head! Off with — "

"Nonsense," Alice said boldly. Katy's eyes widened.

Rean put his hand on her arm. "Consider, my dear. She's only a child!" he said.

Katy shrugged him off and turned to Marek. "Turn them over," she said pointing to the cards.

He did so carefully with one foot, proud to have not one but two important jobs now.

"Get up," said Katy. The cards jumped up, and Katy could see they were the gardeners. They began bowing profusely.

"Enough! What *have* you been doing here?" she demanded.

"May it please Your Majesty," spoke the first one going down on one knee. "we were trying..." Katy walked around the roses as he spoke and noticed a bucket of red paint and brushes. A few of the white roses had been covered in red paint. They had attempted to cover their sins.

"*I* see!" she said. "Off with their heads!" she shouted. She looked at Alice, wanting to keep her close. "Can you play croquet?" Katy asked, forcing her mouth into a smile.

"Yes," the girl answered a bit too enthusiastically.

"Come on, then," said Katy and the procession moved on, with Alice taking step right next to William, the white rabbit.

CHAPTER 49

KATY was anxious to get the game started. She wanted the visitors to be distracted. She wanted to be able to think things through and to get a closer look at this Alice child.

"Get to your places," Katy shouted. The whole crowd hurried about until they were all in place and had their flamingos and hedgehogs. The game began. Katy played along half-heartedly, all the while keeping a close eye on the girl.

Alice was terrible at flamingo croquet. She struggled and fought with the bird and could hardly get a single hit in. Katy saw her talking to someone and hit her hedgehog closer to get a better look. It was Cheshire cat. She felt certain that they were conspiring against her. Of course that cat would be involved. He was loyal to Eisley and practically hated Katy.

Katy stayed nearby, listening and smiling at Alice occasionally. Rean could see what was going on. He was concerned for Alice and knew that Ches could take care of himself. He created a diversion. He managed to get the crowd worked up and terrified of Cheshire's giant floating head.

"Off with his head!" Katy was only too happy to shout out his sentence. There was a great kerfuffle over how to go about cutting off his head when all that they could see of him *was* his head. Katy looked toward Alice.

"He belongs to the Duchess," the girl said, "you'd better ask her about it."

Katy turned to Rean.

"Ches is Eisley's cat," she whispered.

"Perhaps she gave him to the Duchess to keep her company," he replied. Katy nodded. It did sound like something Eisley would do.

"Go fetch the Duchess. She's in prison," she shouted to the closest guard. The games went on. Katy watched as the Duchess was escorted into the courtyard. She went immediately to Alice. She put her arm around her and rested her chin on Alice's shoulder. They walked, intertwined, and spoke in whispers. Katy was certain now that all she feared was true.

She walked closer to hear what they spoke, but it all sounded like nonsense. *It's code,* she thought. Then the Duchess caught sight of her.

"A fine day, Your Majesty," the Duchess said in a weak voice.

"I give you fair warning," Katy stated, "either you or your head must be off...now!"

The Duchess turned and headed into the forest immediately. Katy had to get rid of Alice for a while. She needed to have time to think, to consult with Lutwidge. She turned to Alice.

"Have you seen the Mock Turtle yet?" she asked. When Alice said she hadn't, she directed her there. That would keep her busy for a good while. She had allies there who could watch the girl, and the Mock Turtle took ages telling stories. She would have time to devise a plan. Katy went back to the palace to talk with Lutwidge.

CHAPTER 50

KATY consulted with Lutwidge, who tried to tell her that the conspiracies were all in her head. But she had seen enough to know that there was truth to them. She came up with a plan of her own. When Alice returned, there would be a trial, the most ridiculous trial in the history of trials.

She remembered a rhyme from her childhood.

The Queen of Hearts, she made some tarts,
All on a summer day:
The Knave of Hearts, he stole those tarts
And took them quite away!

She gathered all of the palace staff and laid out her plan. If they wanted to keep their heads, they would follow it. They all agreed the plan was genius, although they were so terrified that they would have agreed that any madness she came up with was genius.

She based the trial on the rhyme. She wanted to look absolutely insane. She wanted to make Alice so appalled with the ridiculousness that she would stand up and speak out against the Queen and hopefully reveal her fellow conspirators in the process.

They brought in the maddest people in the kingdom, including Degrit, now well known as The Mad Hatter, and Nash, known as the March Hare. Katy found it easier now that Degrit was called a different name because he really didn't seem like the same person — that's what she told herself. He was a different person. She was a different person. They rehearsed and prepared for an absurd trial that would infuriate any rational person.

When they heard that Alice was returning, they all ran and jumped into position in the courtroom. Rean wore a white judge's wig under his crown. Marek stood at the front in handcuffs. On a table in front of the King and Queen sat a plate of inviting heart-shaped tarts.

Alice came into the courtroom. Her eyes widened at the scene, and Katy watched her closely throughout the proceedings. Katy grew more and more angry with every passing second. Alice must have had some mushroom in her pockets for at one point she went shooting up to the ceiling, then shrank back to her regular height.

When Katy spoke her next line, "sentence first, verdict afterwards," Alice had finally had enough.

"Stuff and nonsense!" she said loudly.

Katy pushed harder hoping for the truth. "Hold your tongue!" the Queen shouted.

"I won't," Alice shouted back.

Katy stood and pointed her finger at Alice. "Off with her head!" Katy demanded.

"Who cares for *you?*" Alice stared long into Katy's eyes. Something about the way she had said this cut Katy to the core. Then Alice turned to the guards approaching her. "And you're nothing but a pack of cards!" The guards pounced on her and struggled to capture her. They were in a large dog-pile. When the king commanded them to stand, Alice was gone. Vanished. She had found her way back to the Shadowlands.

Katy walked out of the courtroom in the midst of all the chaos. *Who cares for you?* Alice was just a little girl. She didn't want the throne. Katy remembered coming through that mirror. She let herself be in that moment again, and she saw that Alice was just like her. *Who cares for you?*

No one cares for me...not even me.

She was a monster, and she hated herself. She threw down her crown and ran to that bench in the forest. That bench had known her as many different girls, and she was glad that it couldn't speak. As she ran, she tore off her outer dress and was left in just the white slip she wore underneath. Just a girl.

She felt tears rolling down her cheeks. She rubbed her face in astonishment. The last time she had cried real tears had been at Degrit's cottage ages ago.

CHAPTER 51

THE forest was still, and sunlight was streaming through the trees. Katy sat shivering despite the warmth.

"Miss Katy, I have waited long to see you again." She knew the voice immediately.

"Waith!! Oh Waith!!" Katy embraced him.

"Miss Katy, I have watched you from afar since I left, but I've not seen *you*. There has been someone cold and hard wearing your clothes and masquerading as you."

Katy was sobbing now.

"I know..." she said between gasping and crying. "I've become such a horrible person. I don't want this."

Waith rubbed her hand with his tail.

"Katylove, I think it's time to forgive yourself." He paused and looked into her eyes. "It's never too late to start over."

Katy wiped her nose and eyes and looked up at Waith.

"It feels too late," she whispered. Waith caught one of her tears with his tail and held it up for Katy to see.

"Rain...is almost always a sign of new growth." He smiled wide, and

212

Katy laughed at his big toothless grin. Waith patted her leg and slithered away. She watched him go, and as she watched she caught sight of a pair of bright green eyes peering at her through the trees. They were not the eyes of an insane artist. They were the eyes of that boy from so long ago.

She stood and ran hard after him. The tree branches flew past her. She ran faster, determined to catch a moment with her past. Her foot stepped in some sort of rut or hole, and she felt herself falling. When she landed she was looking into a tall mirror in the parlor of a strangely familiar home.

CHAPTER 52

KATHERINE was confused and disoriented. She felt something important slipping away…a dream that you want to remember, but can't seem to hold on to, like trying to hold smoke in your hand. She looked in the tall mirror. She almost didn't recognize herself. There was a depth in her eyes that she didn't remember. A light scar lined her jaw. She ran her finger across it.

"Katherine! Quickly, dearest. Your mother is going to have an absolute fit if she sees you are still in this house. It's time for her guests to arrive!! Come, darling, off with you." Ms. Glass looked closer at her. "Are you all right, love?" Her brows were raised and she looked concerned.

Katherine dusted herself off and stood up. It was gone. That dream that she was trying so desperately to cling to had floated away. Just a tiny wisp of memory lingered; colored lights that danced in a field, and green eyes.

"I'm fine. I think I just slipped and fell." She smiled at Ms. Glass, then gathered her things.

"What's this?" Ms. Glass ran her finger across the scar on her jaw.

"I don't know. Maybe I scraped it when I fell," she said.

"You must try to be more careful," Ms. Glass hugged her and pointed her in the right direction.

Katy walked out into the garden. It was a beautiful day. She felt hopeful. She stood and breathed deeply. The world felt new.

"Hi ya."

Katy whirled around when she heard the voice. A tall boy with wild blond hair and bright green eyes stood before her. She knew him, didn't she?

He smiled. "I'm Trenton. We just moved in next door." He held out his hand. Katy took it.

"I'm Katherine, but you can call me Katy." She smiled at the tiny rebellion she'd just committed by renaming herself. A small blond girl was running toward them.

"That's my little sister, Alice," Trenton said. They all shook hands and made introductions. Katy liked them right away. She felt a renewed sense of hope. Maybe it was time for her to have some real friends, to let someone know her and love her.

"Alice and I are going to hunt fireflies tonight when dusk comes. Do you want to come?" he asked.

"That sounds brilliant! I'd love to," Katy said. She took a deep breath again. The world was new.

ACKNOWLEDGEMENTS

I'D like to thank:

My amazing proofreader, Karen Christakis. Come to think of it, without you, I might not have put any commas in this sentence.

Erin Healy, for your generosity. Your input and encouragement were invaluable.

My friend, Christine, for loving the story enough to create a fleet necklace for me.

Allen Arnold, for your advice, encouragement, and help with cover copy. See you at Comic Con!

My first fans, Debbie, Scarlett, Felicity, Christine, Cathleen, Michelle, and Christi, for reading my early manuscript and encouraging me to keep writing.

My incredible Kickstarter project team, Eli, Mark, Carter, Justin, and Shaun; without you nobody would be reading this book.

Amy Dale is a wife and mother of four. She homeschools, plays and writes music, paints a bit, draws a bit, and writes as much as she can. She's the co-host of the popular video podcast Geeky Faucets.

Amy grew up in Oklahoma but now makes her home in the mountains of Colorado.

Visit her website at www.AmyDale.com